*F*AST TIMES
WITH
*F*RED

Original title: *Justin, Jay-Jay and the Juvenile Dinkent*

Other Scholastic books by Paul Kropp:

Cottage Crazy

FAST TIMES WITH WITH FRED

Original title: *Justin, Jay-Jay and the Juvenile Dinkent*

Paul Kropp

cover by Brian Boyd

Scholastic Canada Ltd.

Scholastic Canada Ltd.
123 Newkirk Road, Richmond Hill, Ontario, Canada L4C 3G5

Scholastic Inc.
730 Broadway, New York, NY 10003, USA

Ashton Scholastic Limited
Private Bag 1, Penrose, Auckland, New Zealand

Ashton Scholastic Pty Limited
PO Box 579, Gosford, NSW 2250, Australia

Scholastic Publications Ltd.
Holly Walk, Leamington Spa, Warwickshire CV32 4LS, England

Canadian Cataloguing in Publication Data

Kropp, Paul, 1948-
    Fast times with Fred

ISBN 0-590-73768-6

I. Title. II. Title: Justin, Jay-Jay and the
juvenile dinkent.

PS8571.R66F38 1990   C813'.54   C90-095574-0
PZ7.K76Fa 1990

6 5 4 3 2 1   Printed in Canada   0 1 2 3 4 5 / 9
                  Manufactured by Gagné Printing

Chapter 1

"I know something you don't know," said my little brother Justin. He delivered this line in the sing-song voice six-year-olds use only when they're trying to bug you.

"I doubt it," I told him. It's hard to imagine that a kid who can't even tie his own shoelaces might know something I don't.

"You don't know everything, Jay-Jay," he challenged me.

"A lot more than you do," I shot back.

Justin took off down the street, kicking at a potato chip bag that was blowing along the sidewalk. He kept kicking and running after the bag until he tripped on his shoelaces and fell onto the front lawn of the old Captain's house.

"Oooah!" Justin screamed.

"Be quiet," I told him. "You're not hurt that much."

"Ooah! I am. I *am* hurt. I could have broken something, you know."

"You can't break bones by falling on grass."

"Yes, you can. Remember when I fell down at Dundas Park? Daddy said I was lucky that I didn't break my leg. So you don't know everything, Jason."

Justin got back to his feet and limped to the corner. That was enough limping to get me a little worried about him. Maybe he had sprained his ankle or even broken something.

I was just about to ask him if he was really hurt when he started running down the sidewalk. It was a miraculous recovery. He does things like that, but of course he's only six. What can you expect from a kid who still believes in the Easter bunny?

I got to the variety store not too long after Justin. I bought my Oh Henry right away, then leaned back against the ice cream freezer to wait for Justin. Sometimes I think he must be the slowest kid in the world. He takes two seconds to get his popsicle out of the freezer, but then he needs ten minutes to figure out how to spend his leftover nickel. He looks at every candy in the store about ten times, picking up half of them for a closer look at the wrapper.

The lady at the cash register was watching Justin as if she expected him to shoplift a chocolate bar or something. For some reason, store clerks look at kids as if we're all potential juvenile delinquents.

"Come on, Justin. Make up your mind."

"How much is this?" he asked me, holding up a sixty-nine cent bar of chocolate.

"You can't afford it. You've only got a nickel left."

"Oh," he said, putting the bar back.

I can never understand why little kids have to act so dumb when they're out in public. It's one thing when you can't add and subtract, it's another thing when you pretend you can't even read a price tag.

"How much is this?"

"Read the sign."

"Oh, five cents. Can I 'ford that?"

"A nickle is worth five cents, right? You've got just enough. Now pay the lady and let's go."

Justin put his fistful of money up on the counter and then waited. The lady put all his coins in the cash register and Justin still waited. I think he would have waited for change all day if I hadn't pulled him out of the store.

On the way back to the house Justin was so busy eating his popsicle that he didn't even watch where he was walking. I thought for sure he was going to walk straight into a fire hydrant.

"Justin," I said, "what were you going to tell me before?"

"When?" he asked, getting closer to the fire hydrant. He still wasn't looking.

4

"When we were going to the store." I figured he'd hit it in two seconds.

"Today?"

"Of course, today! Something that I didn't know."

"Oh, yeah," he said. He skipped around the fire hydrant at the very last second. "I know something you don't know." He had a very satisfied smile on his face.

"Like what?"

"That we're going to get babysitted tonight."

"Babysat, not babysitted," I corrected.

"And the guy who's coming is a juvenile dinkent."

"A juvenile delinquent?"

"Something like that. Daddy told Mommy he tried to get all the good babysitters but they were busy. He has to go to some dinner with Mommy and it's really 'portant so they called up this Fred kid, and Mommy said Daddy's gonna get it if anything goes wrong."

"When'd you find this out?"

"This morning when you were still asleep. *Superfriends* was on TV and you missed it." The last line came at me in his singsong voice. I had an urge to say I was too intelligent to watch those dumb cartoons, but Justin would see through it. Basically, I like to sleep late.

When we got back to the house I finished my Oh Henry and then tried to talk to my dad about the babysitter. I wanted to know if this Fred guy was really a juvenile delinquent or if Justin was only making it up. Unfortunately my father immediately got a blank look on his face, as if his brain were off in California.

"Dad," I said, trying to snap him back.

"Uh — I'll talk to you about it later," he told me. That just meant he wouldn't talk to me about it at all.

Adults are often like that. When they ask a kid a question, they expect an answer right away, and if they don't get one they get mad. But when you're a kid and you ask an adult a question, there's nothing you can do if they don't want to talk to you. Sometimes I wish I could send my father to his room.

That night we ended up having hotdog-and-pickle sandwiches for dinner. Justin and I always end up with hot-dog-and-pickle sandwiches when Mom and Dad are going out for an expensive dinner.

My father stole an extra hotdog, the way he always does, and ate the leftovers from Justin's sandwich as if they were dessert. He said he couldn't be witty and charming without any food in his stomach. I don't know why adults have all these late dinners. If they ate early like the rest of us, they wouldn't have to steal half-eaten hotdogs from their kids.

It wasn't until my father was putting on his blue suit — the one that's getting too tight around the middle but he still won't give it up — that I tried to talk to him again.

"Dad, how come we still have to be babysat?"

"Because you're only ten and not old enough to take care of yourself," he said, trying to tie his tie without a mirror.

"I'm ten-and-a-half and I can take care of myself pretty well. If there was any trouble, we could just call Mrs. Finklestein next door for help."

"You're both still too young," he said, trying to get around my argument. He thought Justin and I were too young to do anything for ourselves. We couldn't play at Gage Park unless he came with us. We couldn't go to the other side of Main Street without getting an adult to cross with us. We were lucky that he let us brush our teeth by ourselves.

And my mother was worse.

"There's no way I'm going to have a ten-year-old and a six-year-old left alone in the house." I heard her voice from way off in the bathroom. I didn't even think she could hear me talking to Dad. I should have known better — my mother has ears like sonar.

"All we need is for one of you to start playing with matches, like that fire in the paper last week. That's all we need," she continued.

I could have told her that neither Justin nor I played with matches, but that would be useless. She'd just invent some other danger for us. There would be some robber who'd come into the house, tie us up and steal the computer and the silver, for example. It didn't matter that we'd never been robbed, that the computer never worked right and that the silver was all tarnished. She'd still worry about it.

"You may think we're being over-protective," my father began — and he was dead right about that — "but you and Justin are just too young and that's all there is to it." By this time he had made a shambles of his tie and had to pull it out and start all over.

"Now with this babysitter," my

mother spoke up again, "you two boys are going to have to be especially careful anyway."

"Fred's a perfectly good kid," Dad broke in. "Maybe he's gone with a bad crowd, but he's basically a good kid. I wouldn't have asked him if I didn't trust him," he told her.

She just gave him The Look. The Look was reserved for those times when my father was acting like a jerk or a show-off or a two-year-old. My father usually got The Look a couple times a day.

"Is Fred a juvenile delinquent?" I asked him.

"How do you know about juvenile delinquents? You're only ten years old."

"Ten-and-a-half. Is he?" I gave him one of my tell-it-to-me-straight looks to convince him I was old enough to handle the truth, and it worked.

"Well, Fred got involved in a silly prank that got him in trouble with the law. But he's all straightened out now."

"Paul, I thought you were kidding this morning. You mean you got an *actual* juvenile delinquent to babysit tonight? How could you?" my mother said in one of her shriekier voices.

"What's a juvenile dinkent?" Justin asked, rushing in from the other room.

"What kind of silly prank?" I asked, always looking for interesting details.

My father seemed a little confused by all these questions being thrown at him at once. All he wanted to do was put on his tie and go to dinner. Now he had three people bugging him about his choice of a babysitter.

"He's had no trouble for two years," he began to reassure my mother. Notice that he answered her first.

"If anything happens tonight, it's your responsibility. I don't even want to go to this dinner now! My stomach is starting to —"

"What's a juvenile dinkent? What is it?" Justin kept on.

With everybody talking at once, I

11

shut up. It's probably a good thing I did, because with me talking too, nobody would have heard the doorbell.

"Could that be him?" Mom said with a little panic in her voice.

"I told him seven-thirty," my father answered.

"He wouldn't show up half an hour early," she decided. "Would he?"

"Jason, go see who it is. Neither of us is dressed," Dad said, standing in the bedroom still without his pants on.

I went down to the little window that looks out on the porch. One look at this guy bouncing up and down on the welcome mat and I knew it had to be Fred. Our babysitter. The juvenile delinquent.

"I think it's him," I yelled upstairs.

"Oh, great," my father said.

"I wanna see the juvenile dinkent," Justin yelled as he ran to open the door.

"It's delinquent, and don't you dare use either of those words," my mother ordered. Then she went off to hide in the bathroom.

Chapter 2

Justin opened the front door and stared at Fred so hard I thought his eyeballs were going to pop out and roll down the steps. Then he let go of the door and it slammed shut right in Fred's face.

Justin thought this was very funny. My father, zipping his pants as he came down the stairs, didn't. He gave Justin a dirty look and opened the door again.

Fred was staring up at the trees outside, talking to no one in particular. "That's all right. That's all right. People laugh at me all the time. I'm used to it."

I guess he'd have to get used to it. One look at Fred was enough to make any ordinary human being smile, and more than enough to throw my little brother into a fit of giggles.

Fred was dressed in a shirt so big it looked as if his body had shrunk, cord pants stained with bleach, a pair of basketball runners with holes for his toes to peek through, and a baseball cap that made his hair stick out sideways. He looked like those kids you see in ads for Save the Children.

But it was his face that was really funny. Justin's giggles must have had something to do with Fred's combination of pimples and freckles, a big mouth and giant ears.

"Come on in, Fred. I'm afraid we weren't expecting you quite so early," my father said.

"I know. My brother kicked me out of the house 'cause his girlfriend was coming over. So I figured I could drive around the streets for a while looking like a juvenile delinquent, or I could just show up a little early."

Justin stopped giggling long enough to blurt out, "He said it! He said it!"

"What did I say?" Fred asked, smiling at Justin. "Is this like one of

14

those game shows where you say the magic word and win a thousand dollars?"

"Dinkent!" Justin cried out.

"Teaching them to swear pretty young, aren't you, sir?"

"Never mind, Fred," my father replied, giving Justin an I'll-talk-to-you-later look. "Come on in."

Fred walked into the hall and looked around at the mirrors and the winding stairs. He acted like a tourist who had just come into a castle, which isn't too surprising since our house has a front hall fit for Queen Elizabeth. It's just the rest of the house that's falling apart.

Fred was so busy looking at the staircase that he walked right into a pillar.

"Oof! These sort of sneak up on you, don't they?"

Justin thought that Fred walking into a pillar was really funny, so he started laughing again. I didn't think it was all that funny. One of Dad's friends had come into the house once and walked right into the same pillar and needed three stitches to fix his face. Of course, he was drunk. But it could be that walking into a pillar was part of coming into the house, like tripping on the throw rug was part of walking into the living room.

Fred tripped on the throw rug.

"I think your house is out to get me," he told my father.

"I keep on meaning to nail down that rug, but I never seem to get around to it. Anyway, you can meet the boys while I'm getting dressed. This is Jason, the serious guy here with the glasses," he said, putting his arm around me. "And this curly-headed one is Justin, who's pretending to be shy." Justin had covered his face with both hands as if to make himself invisible.

"Just make yourself at home," Dad instructed, giving Fred one of the phony smiles he uses with insurance salesmen and friends of my mother.

Fred looked around the living room trying to figure out where to sit down. He felt awkward, the way everybody feels in our living room. The place is decorated like a museum and you expect to see little ropes to keep you from actually sitting down in the rickety old chairs. That didn't stop Justin and me from jumping up and down on the couch, but outsiders always wonder if there's anything safe to sit on. Fred figured he was safest on the piano stool.

"Looks like I'm babysitting you guys tonight. How lucky can you get?"

"Yeah," I agreed, trying to be friendly.

Justin was still pretending to be shy. He always pretends to be shy when he meets somebody new, but it's all a fake. He's about as shy as the guys who sell used cars on TV.

"So you're Justin," Fred began, looking over at him.

Justin smiled behind his hands and peeked at Fred through his fingers.

"You do have curly hair, don't you?" Fred continued. "You're as cute as a girl," he added, making his first serious mistake of the night.

"I am *not* a girl!"

"I didn't say —"

"I'm not a girl and I don't *look* like a girl. I don't think you're a very good babysitter at *all*." Justin had come out from behind his hands and was now pretending he was going to cry.

Fred looked over at me for help, but I just shrugged my shoulders. He'd put his foot in his mouth, so he might as well chew on his toes for a while.

"You can't even tell a girl from a boy! That's pretty dumb. I bet that's why you're a juven—" Justin had to shut up then because my parents were coming down the stairs.

I'm always surprised at how good my parents can look when they're going out someplace. My father's blue suit makes him look like he's got a good job, like running a bank, instead of just teaching high school. And my mother looks like a movie star. There must be a jar in the bathroom that can perform miracles.

Fred seemed impressed by my mother too. "Nice to meet you, ma'am. You know, your husband talks about you quite a lot at school."

"I can just imagine what he says, and you shouldn't believe a word of it. Now I want you to be very, *very* careful with the boys." There was a special emphasis on the second "very," as if Fred didn't look like the kind of person who'd be very careful about anything.

Then Mom went through the baby-sitter briefing routine. She gave Fred instructions on how to do everything except flush the toilet.

"Now, do you have the phone number of where we're going to be?" she asked for the third time.

"Don't worry about a thing," Fred answered.

"Be sure they're both in bed by nine-thirty. There are some cookies on the freezer and Coke in the fridge if you get hungry, and the people next door are home if there's a problem. Don't answer the door for anybody. And if somebody calls on the phone, don't tell them we've gone out. Oh, and be careful of Jason's stomach because too much Coke always makes him sick."

"Mother!" I said.

"Well, it's true, Jason," she went on.

"Bye-bye, kids. Be good," my father said, dragging Mom out the door before she could give Fred still more advice on the dangers that were lurking around the house.

"Daddy," Justin whined while waving, "Fred said I looked like a *girl*."

"Oh, tough beans," my father answered. He said that whenever Justin started to whine about something.

The door slammed shut and the three of us waited in silence for a few seconds while my parents walked to the car. Then Justin broke the silence.

"Are you really a juvenile dinkent?"

Chapter 3

"What's he talking about?" Fred asked, turning to me.

"He wants to know if you're a juvenile delinquent," I said. Fred's eyes bugged out, so I decided to explain. "Dad said you'd been in trouble with the law, so Mom said you were a juvenile delinquent and that's how the whole thing started."

"I can't believe it. I can't believe it," Fred cried, speaking to nobody in particular. "I come into this house and get laughed at, assaulted by a pillar, and accused of being a juvenile delinquent. I ask You, God, do I have to take all this for a measly two bucks an hour?"

Fred was shaking his fist at the ceiling and he seemed so serious in his question that Justin and I shut up. We thought we'd give God a couple seconds to answer, just in case.

"Still not talking up there, eh?" Fred said, looking up. "You know, I try to ring God up almost every day, but the girl at His switchboard always says He's out. I leave my number and say 'God can phone back when He's not so busy,' but He never rings back. Is this any kind of life? Laughed at by people and snubbed by God! What do you think?"

Fred looked at Justin and me with an expression that was supposed to be serious but didn't quite make it.

"I don't know," Justin said.

I was still trying to figure out what kind of babysitter this Fred guy was going to be. Babysitters always come in types: the phony ones who smile a lot even though they hate kids, the smart ones who do it so my Dad will give them a higher mark, the friendly ones who play games for a while, and the dull ones who just stick their noses into a book.

Fred didn't seem to fit into any of those categories.

"Did God make you a juvenile dinkent?" Justin asked.

"No, I did that myself," Fred told him. "With a little help from a guy named Beefy. But I was the one who got caught."

"So you really are a juvenile delinquent," I said. I don't know if I was surprised or impressed or what. Fred wasn't exactly what I had in mind as your typical teenage hoodlum.

"I guess. But it wasn't anything serious, just booby trapping the bathroom at Gage Park, that's all. Really, Your Honour, I promise to go straight from now on. I'm a good boy, Your Honour . . ." Fred raised his left hand, put his right hand on a magazine, and pretended he was on a witness stand.

Justin wasn't impressed. "How'd you booby trap a bathroom?" he asked. "Did the toilet 'splode?"

"No, it was supposed to be like a carwash, only for your bum. But I got caught before I could get it to work. This one pipe didn't fit in just right . . . But look, I'm not supposed to talk about this stuff with little kids. How about right now we do something? What do you guys do around here to keep yourselves amused?"

Justin was pouting because Fred wouldn't give him the details of how to turn a toilet into a bumwash, so I answered. "We watch TV, I guess."

"TV!" Fred shouted, as if I'd told him we liked to stick pickles in our ears.

"What's wrong with watching TV?"

"Nothing, it just turns your brain into a cauliflower. And that's halfway toward turning all of you into a vege-table."

"I am *not* a vegetable and I am not a *girl*," Justin broke in. "I don't like all the names you call me and I don't think you're a very good babysitter."

Fred looked to me for moral support, but there was nothing I could do. Once somebody offends Justin, he has to be careful with everything else he says.

"All I meant was that TV is a waste of time. It does nothing for your mind. It's like that cruddy white bread you buy at the store. You feed it to rats long enough and they'll starve to death. TV's like that for the brain. The more you watch, the more your intelligence starves to death."

"But we're not 'llowed to do anything else," Justin complained. "We can't go to Gage Park and we can't cross the street and we can't play in the backyard —"

I wondered if he was going to go through the whole list of things we couldn't do. It would probably take up the whole evening.

"Okay, okay, I get the idea," Fred broke in. "Turn on the TV."

The three of us went into the TV room and Justin flipped on the set. I checked the program guide, but there wasn't much to choose from at seven-thirty: *The Dating Game*, prehistoric

Mary Tyler Moore shows, a super-boring talk show on the educational channel, and *The Brady Bunch*. I chose the best of them.

"*The Brady Bunch?*" Fred yelled.

"My favourite show," Justin said, even though it wasn't. Justin has about fifty favourite shows, probably because he doesn't know the difference between just liking a show and having it as his favourite.

"I can't stand it!" Fred cried, running to the TV and pushing the off button.

"I wanna watch *The Brady Bunch*," Justin whined. It was a really good whine, I have to admit.

"Please, Justin, anything but that," Fred begged. "I can handle almost any show. I can watch *Three's Company* or *Mr. Rogers* or even *Green Acres*, but not *The Brady Bunch*. You know, I even made up a song about that."

"About what?" Justin asked.

"*The Brady Bunch*," Fred told him.

"You want to hear it? I don't know if I can remember all the verses, but —"

"You can sing, Fred?" I asked.

"Sure I can. At least as good as Weird Al Yankovic — and my song is funnier than his. Listen."

Fred pulled a harmonica out his shirt pocket, tooted a note or two, and then began to sing in the most awful, out-of-tune voice I have ever heard.

> Oh, on TV there's this bunch
>   they call the Bradys,
> Who smile so much they almost
>   make you feel
> That together they're the world's
>   most perfect family,
> But they just aren't real.
> The Brady Bunch, oh, the
>   Brady Bunch,
> Yeah, the Brady Bunch, ooh,
>   the Brady Bunch,
> Ugh, the Brady Bunch — burp —
>   the Brady Bunch,
> Oh, I just can't stand the . . .
> The Brady Bunch.

Oh, I can always handle Barney
  and Betty Rubble,
And the war games of that maniac,
  G.I. Joe,
I can even veg while Gilligan gets
  in trouble,
But the Bradys, they just have to go.
  The Brady Bunch, oh, the Brady Bunch,
Yeah, the Brady Bunch, ooh,
  the Brady Bunch,
Ugh, the Brady Bunch — burp —
  the Brady Bunch,
Oh, I just can't stand the . . .
The Brady Bunch.

     There were a lot more repeats of the words "the Brady Bunch" and some tooting on the harmonica in between. When Fred was finally finished, Justin clapped his hands like crazy. I preferred to sit on mine. The only part of the whole song that was in tune came when Fred burped in the chorus. Fred can do a really loud burp.

     "Sing some more, Fred. You're the first babysitter we ever had who sang to us," Justin said.

"If you call that singing," I added. I wondered if Fred was a New Wave juvenile delinquent.

"Of course it's singing," Fred shot back. "Trouble is, that's the only song I've got in my head right now. I've got the other ones back at my brother's place."

"The other heads?" I suggested.

"No, Jason, the other songs. I've got about a hundred songs all written down in a book. I could sing them all night," he said.

"Oh, great," I muttered under my breath.

"I wanna hear them all," Justin piped up. He has an enthusiasm for some things which makes no sense at all to me.

"It beats watching TV," Fred agreed. "I could just drive over to my brother's place and pick up the song book. Then you could have the musical evening of your short little lives — a concert with 'Weird Fred and his Hapless Harmonica.' What could be better than that?"

I could think of a few things, but decided to keep my mouth shut.

"Who's going to babysit us when you go?" Justin asked, suddenly worried at the idea of being left alone.

"You guys can come with me. I've got my truck parked right out front."

"A truck!" Justin said, his eyes glowing.

"Oh, no," I said, because somebody had to say something sensible. "We're not allowed to do that."

"He's got a *truck*, Jay-Jay," my little brother said, as if that should change my mind.

"It's only a ten minute drive," Fred told me.

"We'd all get in trouble," I replied. Somebody had to keep us out of trouble and I knew it wouldn't be Fred. What if Justin got hurt? What if *I* got hurt?

"No, we won't," Justin said. "Remember the babysitter who took us to see *The Shaggy D.A.*? You remember him, don't you, Jason? He had the car with the 'lectric windows that went up and down and all you had to do was push a button. We didn't get into trouble when we went for a ride in *his* car."

That was true — but this was more complicated. Going to see *The Shaggy D.A.* with the son of a church minister wasn't quite the same thing as going for a joyride with a juvenile delinquent, even if Fred was a reformed juvenile delinquent. But how could I explain this to Justin with Fred sitting right there?

"Look, we'll be back here at the house in less than half an hour. Your parents will never even know we've gone out. Besides, I don't think your dad would mind," Fred told me.

"Come on, Jason. Don't be such a fraidy-cat," Justin said.

"I'm not a fraidy-cat," I tried to explain. "It's just that we're not supposed to go out. Suppose they call the house to check on us and nobody's home? They'll be worried."

"They're always worried about us,"

Justin said, and I couldn't disagree with that. "I wanna go for a ride in Fred's truck. Is it a *big* truck?"

"Oh, the biggest," Fred said, though I knew he was exaggerating.

The look I got from Justin at that point told me I might as well give in. He looked determined, the way only a six-year-old can look determined.

So — despite the rules, despite the fact that we could get in trouble, despite the fact that Fred was a juvenile delinquent, and despite the fact that I didn't like Fred's singing anyhow — I said okay.

That was *my* first mistake of the night.

Chapter 4

It took us quite a while to get out of the house. First Justin couldn't find his shoes, then he couldn't find his jacket, then he managed to put his jacket on but couldn't get his shoes on, then he asked me to tie his shoes, and finally he got Fred to zip up his jacket. It takes Justin almost as long to get ready to go outside as it takes an astronaut to get ready to go to the moon.

"Does he always take this long?" Fred asked me.

"You should see him in winter," I told him.

It was getting dark when we got outside, and I wondered if my decision to go along for the ride was a good one. Mrs. Finklestein was sitting on her porch, staring at Fred as if he were a creature from another galaxy. I knew she'd tell my mom we went out with a spaceman, and then Mom would ask me about it and I'd have to tell the truth and we'd all get in trouble.

But I figured it was too late to back out now, so I didn't say anything. I did go back in the house and stick a few dollars in my pocket, though. Just in case.

"Here it is." Fred pointed proudly to his truck.

"It's not the *biggest*," Justin replied, and he was quite right.

"Well, it's the biggest truck I've ever had."

Justin couldn't argue with that and neither could I. The most interesting thing about the truck wasn't its size anyway. What amazed me was the colour of it. The whole truck seemed to be covered with rust.

Fred hopped up on the back of the pickup and walked around in the box.

"I've got to get some sheet metal to cover up these holes, but otherwise it's a great truck. You want to climb up?" he asked Justin.

"How come it smells like poo?" Justin asked, climbing onto the rear of the truck.

At first I thought he was cracking up. Then I moved in closer and I could smell it too. The back of Fred's truck smelled like a toilet.

"It's manure that I deliver on weekends," Fred explained.

"What's manure?" Justin asked.

"Uh — horse dung, you know, plop — uh —" Fred looked to me for help.

"It's horse poo, Justin."

"That's what I said," Justin replied angrily as he jumped off the truck. "Why do you drive around with poo in your truck?"

"Would you believe me if I told you that people use it in their gardens? It improves the nitrogen content of the soil, adds calcium, phosphorous and a dozen other minerals."

Justin looked over at me to see if he

should believe this or not. I nodded yes, really impressed by the stuff about nitrogen content.

"I already knew that," Justin said, using one of his favourite lines.

"Oh, sure, sure," I told him.

Fred looked up at the sky as if he was ready to make one of his long-distance calls to God. I knew how he felt.

The three of us climbed into the cab of the truck from the passenger door because the driver's door was wired shut. The inside of the cab was a mess. There were wires all over the floor, a lot of holes in the dashboard where there should have been meters and switches, and two huge speakers in separate boxes.

"I know it looks pretty messy," Fred apologized, "but it's a lot like me. Sort of broken down and in the process of being fixed up. Not much in here works quite the way it should, except for the tape deck. Just wait till you hear the tape deck."

We heard the tape deck. So did

everybody else on the street. I just saw the back of Mrs. Finklestein as she rushed in to phone the police. Even the deaf old Captain came out on his porch to see about the noise.

"Turn it down," Justin shouted, his hands clamped over his ears.

"We're going to get in trouble," I yelled over the noise.

"What's the matter?" Fred shouted back. "You guys don't appreciate music or something?"

I really like music, but that wasn't the problem. The problem was whether the police would arrive and arrest us or whether my eardrums would burst first. I reached forward and turned down the tape deck.

"Now you guys have got to help me start the truck," Fred announced when we could all hear again.

I wondered if that meant we'd have to get outside and turn a crank like in an old movie. The truck was in such lousy shape I was ready to believe anything.

"When I turn the starter, you've got to say the magic words 'outrageous curmudgeon,'" Fred explained.

I knew right away that he was kidding, but Justin was taken in by every word. Fred turned the key, the starter growled like some creature in a horror movie, and nothing happened.

"See. You didn't say 'outrageous curmudgeon,' so the truck wouldn't start. Now say it!"

Fred turned the key again and Justin shouted over the grinding engine, "Rageous cushion!"

"Keep on shouting," Fred encouraged him.

"Rageous cushion! Rageous cursin! Rageous person! Rageous! Ragus!"

"Ragu spaghetti sauce," I said, making fun of the whole thing.

Justin laughed and Fred yelled. But then the most amazing thing happened — the truck started.

"Jay-Jay *did* it!" Justin shouted.

And maybe I did.

Fred pumped up and down on the gas pedal to keep the engine from stalling. That kept the motor going, but it also produced a tremendous cloud of smoke.

"Are we on *fire*?" Justin asked.

"It burns a little oil," Fred explained.

"Are you a safe driver, Fred?" I ventured as he pulled the truck out into the street.

"A safe driver! I've almost got a chauffeur's licence. I've been driving cars and trucks ever since I was twelve," he bragged.

"That's illegal," I said.

"I used to drive through the fields of my old man's farm, Mr. Prosecutor," Fred told me.

"Daddy says you've got to be sixteen to drive. I can drive in — uh —" Justin started counting on his fingers.

"Ten years," I said to help him out.

"You don't have to help me, Jason. I can figure it out *myself*," he said to me.

Then, turning to Fred, he repeated my figure. "I can drive in ten years."

"That's great." Fred smiled, winning Justin over to his side even more firmly. I was starting to feel like a curmudgeon myself.

"How fast are you going?" I asked.

"Don't know. The speedometer's broken."

"Maybe you should slow down," I suggested.

"Don't slow down . . . this is fun!" Justin yelled. He looked both happy and scared, but mostly happy, like the people who stagger off a roller coaster ride.

Gage Park went whizzing by the window as we headed along Main. We passed the old movie theatre that's been closed ever since we saw *Fantasia* and Justin spilled his extra-large Coke all over the floor. Then we passed the dentist's office, where the nurse shows you how to use dental floss so you've got one more thing to feel guilty about when you never even look at the dental floss again until the day before your next appointment.

And I knew what was coming next.

"Stop the truck! Stop the truck. This is a 'mergency! Stop the truck!" Justin screamed.

Fred pulled the truck across three lanes of traffic and into a parking spot so fast I was sure we were going to hit two cars and a fire hydrant. We didn't. Fred drives just the way Justin walks.

"Wow!" Justin said, with his usual flair for words.

"What's the matter?" Fred asked carefully, a little shaken by his own fast parking job.

"McDonald's is up ahead and I'm hungry," Justin announced.

"Is that all?" Fred snapped. I think he was pretty angry at that point.

"For Justin it's enough," I explained.

"I want some french fries and a Big Mac," Justin said.

"Well, I haven't got any money," Fred told him.

"Jason does. Jason *always* has money, don't you, Jason?"

"Do you?" Fred asked.

"Of course," I told him.

"How much?"

"None of your business," I said firmly.

"He's got almost a thousand dollars," Justin said. Actually, Justin doesn't know the difference between hundreds and thousands, so he gets the figures all mixed up.

"Really?" Fred seemed impressed.

"Of course not," I said, amazed that Fred might really believe Justin. "I've got $178.45."

"That's more money than I've ever had in my whole life — and you're only ten years old," Fred said, staring at me.

"Ten-and-a-half," I told him. I figured he was just trying to butter me up.

"How much have you got with you?" he asked.

"A little bit," I said.

"Stop being a cheapskate, Jason. I

42

want to get a Big Mac 'cause I'm hungry. We only had hotdog-and-pickle sandwiches for dinner, you know," Justin whined.

I thought about that for a second and realized I was hungry too. Maybe a stop at McDonald's wouldn't be such a bad idea.

"Okay, we can go to McDonald's," I told the two of them. "You can have your Big Mac, Justin, and I'll let you have some of my fries. And Fred, you can have anything you want so long as it doesn't cost more than a dollar. That's the deal."

"Wow, generous!" Fred shot back.

"For a crack like that," I informed him, "you can pay me back out of your babysitting money."

"Jason, when you grow up you should become the president of a bank," Fred told me.

"Thanks," I said. "But why do I have to wait till I grow up?"

Chapter 5

"I'd like to say right now that I object to going to McDonald's," Fred announced as he bounced the truck over the speed bumps in the parking lot. "We could just as easily go down to Hutch's and get some real food."

"I never even heard of Hutch's," Justin said. "And I want a Big Mac."

Fred kept on trying. "Don't you realize that McDonald's hamburgers have no taste? If it weren't for the special sauce, Ronald McDonald would be out selling vacuum cleaners door-to-door."

"I don't care," Justin said. "I *like* special sauce. I want a Big Mac and I want a Ronald McDonald vaccuum cleaner too."

If Fred had a car telephone, he could have put in another call to God. As it was, he just looked up at the sky. There was nothing I could do to make Justin more sensible. When a little kid gets his mind stuck on a Big Mac, there's not much anyone can do to unglue it.

Fred turned off the truck and the silence made a ringing noise in my ears.

"What do you want to eat, Fred?" I said. I was ready to go in and handle the order for all of us. At least that way I could make sure they didn't spend too much of my money.

"We'll all go in," Fred told me.

"Oh, good. I wanna play in the McDonaldland playground," Justin said.

"You're too old for that," I told him.

"Ronald McDonald plays there and he's as old as Daddy," Justin shot back.

"Ronald McDonald is demented," Fred replied.

"Ronald McDonald is *not* dented! Your *truck* is dented. People can't get dented," Justin lectured.

Fred and I exchanged a look.

When we got inside, Justin took off for the playground while Fred and I went to the line-up at the counter. There were only two people ahead of us, which wasn't too bad compared with the line-up at dinner time. Sometimes I wonder why they call McDonald's a fast-food restaurant. Faster than what?

The chubby girl who was looking after our line wasn't going to lose any weight at the speed she filled the orders. She was bulging out of her McDonald's uniform in several places. From the look in Fred's eyes, though, I think he approved of all the bulges. In fact, he was so busy looking at her bulges that he ended up walking right into me.

"Oof," he said, I think because my elbow caught him in a sensitive spot. "You've got sharp bones, Jason."

"And you should watch where you're walking," I told him.

"May I take your order?" the girl asked.

"Oh, yes, yes," Fred told her in a voice I hadn't heard before. "You can take my order anywhere you want, just keep it on a leash so it doesn't get away."

Fred smiled. The girl gave him a look as if *she* wanted to leave a telephone message with God. I didn't think Fred's joke was that bad — not enough to get me rolling on the floor, but not bad.

The girl didn't even smile. "May I take your order?" she repeated.

"What's a nice girl like you doing in a place like this?" Fred was using a voice that was supposed to sound sexy but didn't quite make it.

"I work here. Now could I take your order?"

Fred was impressing this girl about as much as his truck impressed me. I decided to help out.

"We'd like a Big Mac, large fries, and — what do you want, Fred?"

For a second I thought he might actually lean over the counter and tell the girl, "You, my dear," and make a total fool of himself. But he didn't.

"Uh — a Quarter Pounder," he said.

I realized that Fred's order had just gone way over my one dollar limit, but I decided not to embarrass him in front of the girl. I waited until she went off to put the order together.

"You could have ordered something cheaper," I whispered.

"Give me a break. I haven't eaten anything all day," he whispered back.

"Why not?"

"My brother doesn't like me eating up his food. The only thing I've got left is potatoes. I won't have any money to buy food until your dad pays me tonight."

I looked at Fred with new eyes. I don't think I'd ever met anybody so poor he couldn't even eat. Maybe that's why his body couldn't quite fill up his clothes.

The McDonald's girl returned with our order and began to stuff it into a bag. "Is there anything else you'd like?" she asked.

"Vinegar and ketchup, please," I said.

"And your phone number," Fred added, smiling at her with all his might.

I was thinking Fred could use a little

advice on how to talk to girls, but I didn't have a chance to get started. A guy came up next to us at the counter and stopped Fred cold.

"This guy bugging you, Carla?" I heard as I was counting out the money to pay for the food.

I looked around to see where the voice was coming from. At first I saw nothing but a gigantic T-shirt and a pair of hairy armpits. Then I looked up and realized there was, in fact, a head on top of the T-shirt. It was a head that ought to have belonged to King Kong Bundy on the Saturday wrestling show.

Fred was strangely quiet. I turned and saw him with his mouth open, staring at the guy with hairy armpits. I think he was trying to say something intelligent, like "Uunnh," but there wasn't any sound coming out of his mouth.

"Leave him alone, Beefy," the McDonald's girl said to the giant next to us. It seemed to me I'd heard the name someplace before.

"I — uh —" Fred managed to say. I think this was supposed to be the start of a sentence.

"If you like your face the way it is, Fred," the big guy said, "you better take it someplace else. Fast."

Beefy was staring at Fred. Fred was staring at Beefy. I was staring back and forth at the two of them, wondering what a reasonable kid was supposed to say at a time like this. But an unreasonable kid broke in before I could say a word.

"Where are my french fries?" Justin asked nobody in particular. When he didn't get an answer, he tried it again, this time louder. "*Where* are my french fries?"

"Uh — they're coming, Justin," Fred told him, finally able to say something. "Or — uh — no, they're not," he quickly added on, looking at Beefy. "The frier went wild and burned all the french fries. You don't want burnt fries, do you?"

"I want *regular* fries!" Justin whined. It was one of those whines that could build up into a real cry if Justin worked on it a little more.

"No regular fries here," Fred told him. "C'mon, I know another place we can get some."

"But, Fred —" I began.

"No buts," Fred told me, pushing Justin and me away from the counter. "We'll talk about it later."

"But —"

"Cancel the order," Fred shouted to the McDonald's girl. "Cancel everything."

Beefy was standing by the order counter with a smile on his face as big as the smile on the Hamburgler statue at his side. The McDonald's girl was looking at us, holding out her hand to me. If only Fred had stopped pulling us out the door, I could have saved us a lot of grief. But he had a strong grip and he was bigger than us — though not by much.

"Fred, you're *hurting* me," Justin said.

"No, I'm not. I'm just helping you walk faster," Fred told him.

"Ooah. Don't push! I just want my french fries," Justin kept on.

"I told you, the machine is burning them up. They only have charcoal fries here, nothing but carbonized potatoes! We'll go to some other McDonald's. We'll go to the McDonald's with the *big* playground, the one in Grimsby. Won't that be nice?" Fred asked with a sickly smile on his face. By this time he had dragged us right back to the truck.

"But I'm hungry *now*," Justin whined.

"Yeah, but now isn't a good time. Now is a very unhealthy time — maybe not for you, but for some of us. You don't want to see your babysitter turned into a mass of boneless chuck, do you?"

"Yeah!" Justin yelled. "I want to see it. And I want my french fries."

"You'll get them soon," Fred told

him, annoyed. We were all in the truck and the thing wouldn't start again. "You'll get them as soon as —" But the starter just ground away.

"You need the magic word," Justin said, simply enough.

"I need more than that," Fred told him.

"Rageous cushion, ragu cushion, spaghetti cushion, pin cushion," Justin chanted.

Fred turned the key one last time just as Justin shouted, "Ragu spaghetti sauce."

And the truck started. Fred threw it into reverse, the gears ground out a loud and prolonged protest, and we were off.

"Fred," I began again.

"Yeah, what is it?" he said.

"You know back at McDonald's where we left the food behind?"

"Yeah."

"Well, we left the money behind too. I *paid* for all that."

"Why didn't you get the money back before we left?"

"Because some teenage jerk was pulling me out the door," I shot back.

"Oh," he mumbled. "Sorry."

"But how are we gonna buy french fries now?" Justin whined. "You promised me french fries and now I'm *really* hungry. I'm gonna die of starvation."

"Stop exaggerating, Justin," I told him. "McDonald's french fries couldn't save anybody from starvation."

"Yes, they could. They could save me. You don't know everything, Jason," he said.

"Look, you two, stop fighting. I'll get you both french fries and anything else you want. Just stick with me, guys. I've got an idea."

Chapter 6

Five minutes later Fred was happily driving down Burlington Street. The tape deck was blaring out some strange song about fish heads. Justin was busy getting his fingers stuck in holes under the dashboard. I figured it was as good a time as any to ask Fred why he was so scared of Beefy.

"Fred, why'd you run away from the guy at McDonald's?"

"I didn't run away, Jason. I made a strategic retreat," he explained.

"What kind of treat?" Justin asked.

"A *re*treat, Justin," I sighed. "But don't you think that was a little — well, chicken?" I asked Fred.

"Chicken's not a treat," Justin said. "Candy's a treat. Ice cream's a treat if it's got chocolate sauce . . ."

Justin's list kept going on and on, so

I did the only sensible thing. I said, "I give up," and decided to talk to Fred about it later.

"So did I," Fred said quietly.

The truck had reached old Beach Road and was bouncing over the potholes like a metal kangaroo. Justin seemed to enjoy the bouncing far more than my stomach did.

"Don't you think we're going too fast?" I asked Fred.

"Maybe. Like I said, the speedometer's broken so I don't know."

"Why not slow down before you break your truck?" I could have added something like "or before I throw up," but I figured I'd keep that to myself.

"No, don't slow down, Fred. This is fun!" Justin yelled. If he said that one more time I really would throw up.

"This is dangerous," I warned both of them.

"That's what my mother used to say when my father drove," Fred replied.

"Then what did your father do?"

"Drove even faster. Eventually my mother gave up and moved out."

"Is that when you became a juvenile delinquent?" I asked.

"No, later," Fred answered, eyes on the road. "Hold tight."

He steered quickly to the left to avoid a pothole, then pulled back to the right to avoid a ditch. Justin screamed — just to add to the confusion — and the truck jumped up in the air after hitting a speed bump.

"We're here," Fred announced as he pulled the truck into Hutch's parking lot.

"But my stomach is back there," I said.

"You can't lose your stomach, Jason. It's 'tached," Justin corrected me.

Fred and I exchanged a look. The look said something like "Six-year-olds!" Only with a million exclamation marks.

"Okay, you two, when we get inside I'll do the ordering and you guys keep your mouths shut. After you get the hamburgers and shakes, take them out here to the truck. No matter what happens, get the food to the truck. Got it?"

"Got it."

"Got it."

We could smell the grease of cooking hamburgers even before we got into the restaurant. Hutch's is a kind of prehistoric McDonald's that was serving hamburgers to people back when they took trolleys to get down to the beach and swim. Of course, I've never even seen a trolley and you'd have to go to the hospital if you tried to swim at the beach these days, but Hutch's still serves hamburgers. My father says Hutch's makes the best hamburgers in town, but I prefer Harvey's myself.

Fred got in a line that led to a window with *Hamburgs/Drinks* marked on the wall over it. Justin and I stood beside him and watched him make funny faces while we waited. He finally made it to the window and ordered three hamburgers and three milkshakes.

I did a fast calculation and knew

that Fred would need $5.75 for the food, and maybe more for tax. I also knew that anything over fifty cents meant financial ruin for the three of us. I tried to catch his eye to warn him, but he just bounced up and down at the window, a silly smile on his face.

When the food arrived, Fred passed the hamburgers and shakes down to Justin and me. He had just handed down the last milkshake when something really strange happened. He fell to the floor like a piece of limp spaghetti. Everybody in line jumped back to make a circle around him. Fred had fainted!

I looked over at Justin and saw that his mouth had dropped open. For once he was at a loss for words. So was I.

"Someone help this boy," a lady in the crowd cried out.

By this time a man from behind the hamburger window had moved to the front and was helplessly looking at Fred. He turned to the lady and asked, "What should I do?"

"I don't know," she said. "Maybe mouth-to-mouth resuscitaion?"

The hamburger man looked at the lady, then down at Fred. Fred was still out cold, but now his mouth had fallen open and his tongue was dangling out the side. He looked . . . well, revolting.

"Maybe we should just wait for the ambulance," the man said.

"If this boy dies —" the lady began.

"Somebody save Fred," Justin let out in one of his great wails.

The adults were finally moved by Justin's cry. The guy from behind the counter grunted, wiped his mouth on his sleeve, and bent down over Fred.

"Pinch his nose first," the lady yelled over Justin's crying. Then the whole crowd began shouting advice.

But before the man could follow any of the instructions, Fred's eyes opened. He stared at the crowd of people with a how-did-I-get-here look. Then he rolled over on his elbow and sat up a little.

The crowd let out a sigh of relief and everybody started talking.

"Are you all right?" the hamburger man asked Fred.

"I think so. Gosh, I'm sorry. I must have forgotten to take my medicine. Really, I haven't fainted like that in years. I'm so sorry." His voice was weak and shaky.

"He'll be all right now," the lady said with some authority.

"Gosh, it's so embarrassing," Fred sighed.

"You just take it easy now. I'd better get back to work." The hamburger man patted Fred on the shoulder as if he were a package with *Fragile* stamped all over it.

Fred walked out to the truck very slowly, the eyes of the crowd following him in case he fell down again. Justin and I walked a fair distance behind him and didn't say a word until we reached the truck.

Then Fred turned to us and

demanded in his usual voice, "Where's the food?"

"What food?" I said.

"Three hamburgers and three milkshakes, guys. I thought I told you to bring the stuff to the truck no matter what."

"But you got sick and we —"

"We thought you were going to *die*," Justin interrupted.

"That was all just an act. I call it 'the fake fainting fit.' You fall limp on the floor and they forget all about the bill."

"A fake fainting fit?" Justin said, using the "f's" to spray us all.

"Cut it out, will ya?" Fred told him, wiping his face. "Where's the food?"

"We left it inside," I muttered, embarrassed to have forgotten the food and Fred's instructions.

"You left it inside!"

"We thought you were going to die," Justin said again.

Fred gave him a look so full of disgust that even Justin could see it. He started screwing up his face and I knew he was going to cry.

"Don't get mad at Justin," I told Fred. It wasn't fair to blame him for forgetting the food. Or me either.

"I'm not mad, I'm just — exasperated."

"Does that mean you're going to faint again?" Justin asked, looking more afraid than upset.

"No, it means we're all going to stay hungry," Fred told him, though in my opinion that didn't explain "exasperated" very well.

"We could go back inside and get the stuff," I offered.

"Are you kidding? We better get out of hcre before that lady comes over to check my blood pressure," Fred replied, turning the key to start the truck. The truck, of course, didn't start.

So there we sat. I was embarrassed, Fred was even more exasperated than before, Justin was still afraid that Fred would die, and the truck wouldn't start. "You need spaghetti sauce," I whispered.

"Oh, yeah," Fred replied. "Justin, can you help me start the truck?"

Justin was more than ready to help. "Ragu spaghetti sauce," he chanted, smiling at the magic words.

Fred tried the starter again and the truck sputtered into life. With an awful grinding of gears, he put the truck into reverse and we backed out of the parking lot.

"Fred," Justin said quietly. It was the voice he used whenever he wanted to get something from my dad. I could tell from the voice what was coming.

"Yeah?" Fred replied. I think he was still exasperated.

"Fred," Justin said, his voice so sweet and innocent that he could probably have asked for the moon and had somebody go up to get it for him, "I'm still a *teensy* bit hungry."

Chapter 7

"I've got another idea," Fred told the two of us. "How about I *make* you guys some french fries and onion rings? How about that, eh?" he asked, getting that crazy grin back on his face.

"You, Fred?" I asked.

"You can cook?" Justin echoed.

"Yeah, sure," he said. "We're not too far from my brother's house and he ought to be gone by now, so what say we stop off there and make up some real food? None of these prepackaged, prefrozen, predigested McDonaldized fries. We'll have genuine fries and rings created by your master chef, me."

"Fred's fries," Justin said, obviously happy with the idea. "I want some Fred's fries."

I let Justin repeat his joke another ten times before I finally told him to shut up. By that time we were racing down old Beach Road as if it were a superhighway. It only took about three minutes at that speed to reach Fred's brother's house — that is, if you could call it a house.

"This is where you *live*?" Justin asked. He was staring at a house that was about the size of an old summer cottage. The chimney was leaning like the Tower of Pisa and the whole place was at a tilt, as if the wind had pushed it sideways.

"It looks like our garage," Justin said.

"Yeah, but that's only the outside," Fred told him. "Wait till you see the inside."

"So it's fixed up really nice inside?" I asked.

"No, it's a dump," Fred replied.

He wasn't kidding.

There was a lot of old overstuffed furniture inside, the nice comfy kind we used to have before my mother went wild on antiques. Justin always loved that old furniture and his eyes lit up when he saw this stuff. He spotted a big purple couch, raced over and bounced down on it. The couch responded by bouncing him back up and he started to laugh. "I *like* this place, Fred."

"I'm glad," Fred told him. "But go easy on my bed."

"This is your bed?" Justin asked. I think he was really amazed by this.

"Yeah. So don't give it any more lumps than it already has. I've got to sleep on it till my inheritance comes in."

"What's a 'heritance?" Justin asked.

"Fred's just kidding," I told him.

"What's a 'heritance?" he asked again, turning to Fred this time.

"I'm going to get a million dollars from my rich Uncle Ebenezer when he dies — but there's a minor problem. He's not dead yet." Fred looked at Justin seriously, but he winked at me.

"And he's only twenty-two, so you've got a long wait," I added.

"How d'you know that, Jason?" Justin asked.

"Because I know everything," I said simply. For once I think Justin almost believed me.

We went out to the kitchen and Fred opened the back door to let in some air. He also let in a bunch of sand flies, but he didn't seem too concerned about that. He was busy talking to himself, getting things together for the french fries and onion rings. "Let's see, potatoes . . . lots of potatoes . . . onions, my brother won't mind if I borrow a few onions . . . and the oil . . . an egg. I wonder if he's got an egg in the fridge . . . oooh, something in the fridge has been dead for a long time . . . yeah, here's an egg. Now all I need is a coat hanger."

Justin and I were sitting on either side of the kitchen table watching Fred at work. Or at least I was watching. Justin had found an old handmixer and was busy trying to break it. He had almost succeeded when the last part of

Fred's mumbling made me curious. "A coat hanger?"

"For the onion rings," Fred replied.

"Oh," I said, as if that made some kind of sense. Nothing that had happened since Fred came over to babysit had made much sense. But I was beginning to feel all right about that. Maybe life shouldn't make sense all the time. Maybe sometimes it should just be crazy, and fun.

Fred poured a lot of cooking oil from a big metal can into a pan on the stove. Then he took a match, lit the gas under the pan, and handed me a bunch of potatoes.

"You ever peel potatoes?" he asked me.

"I will!" Justin broke in, trying to get his finger out of the handmixer.

"You can help with the onion rings, Justin," Fred told him. "This job requires Jason's brainpower."

"Peeling potatoes?" I wondered.

"Yeah, you do it like this," Fred told

me. Then he took a potato peeler and produced a skinless potato in about thirty seconds. That looked easy enough, so I began doing what Fred had done, only it took me a little longer — like about five minutes for the first potato. Maybe brainpower wasn't quite as important for this job as Fred had made out.

Justin and Fred were busy mixing up the batter for the onion rings. Then Fred took three giant onions and began to cut them up in front of Justin, telling some incredible story about his Aunt Elsie and how she died when attacked by a wild chicken. By the time the onions and the Aunt Elsie story were finished, both of them were crying. But I think it was the onions that did it.

Fred came back over to finish up the potatoes after he had the onions ready to go. In just a couple minutes he had a pile of hand-cut french fries sitting in front of us. By then the oil on the stove was smoking and Fred told the two of us to get back by the table.

"Is it gonna 'splode?" Justin asked.

"*Ex*plode, Justin," I said.

"That's what I said. Is it gonna 'splode?" he asked Fred.

"It might," Fred told him. "Put your head down on the table and cover your ears while I put the french fries in."

Justin was dumb enough to do just what Fred told him. I shook my head and Fred gave me a wink. The potatoes made the oil sputter and pop, but there was no hint of an explosion.

"Can I look now?" Justin asked, peeking with one eye already.

"Yeah, it's safe," Fred told him. He was busy dipping the onion rings in the batter, then tossing them into the boiling oil. Every so often some oil would pop out and burn him and he would cry out with swear words I had never heard before — things like "Blessed Oliver Plunkett!!" and "Dirty Ratzumphratz!!" I thought that was pretty good, since everybody else I know can only swear with words that start with "s" and "f."

In five minutes the onion rings and french fries were done. Fred used the coat hanger to pull the onion rings out of the hot oil, then scooped out the french fries with a spoon.

"Success!" he cried, salting the steaming pile of fries and rings.

"Ooah!" Justin cried. "Fred's fries are *too* hot."

"No, Fred's fries are always perfect," Fred replied, "but sometimes you have to wait a little before you eat them. I'll get you some water."

"Don't you have Coke?" Justin asked.

"This is better," Fred told him. "Coke will rot out your teeth and your brains. But Fred's exclusive mineral water will keep you alive to a hundred and five." He filled three glasses from the cold water tap.

"This is great min'ral water," Justin said.

"And good french fries," I told him. "They taste sort of oniony though."

"That's okay. They're all natural, totally fresh and unconditionally guaranteed. I should have thought of this earlier and not wasted our time at McDonald's and Hutch's."

"Our time and *my* money," I said. "Why'd we have to run away, Fred?"

"That guy Beefy wants to turn my face into cauliflower," Fred explained.

"You can't turn a face into a flower," Justin said.

"That means he wants to beat me up," Fred told him.

"Yeah, but he couldn't hit you in McDonald's," I pointed out.

"He might try," Fred replied.

"Why would he? What's the problem between you two anyhow?"

"It's a long story."

"I wanna hear the story," Justin yelled. "I *like* your stories."

"Well, mostly it goes back to grade five. Beefy and I used to live on the same street, see. It's called Dorrance Street and it's so far on the wrong side of the tracks they don't even have tracks, if you know what I mean. Anyway, I was still living with my mother at the time and she was sort of living with my father, except he was in jail, so you can see that the family didn't spend a lot of time together watching *The Brady Bunch* on TV. When I was younger I was a little sensitive about all this — my dad in jail and my mom on welfare and all that. And Beefy used to bug me about it. One day he called my mother a bag lady and I went wild on him. I broke his nose," Fred concluded.

"*You* broke *his* nose?" I asked.

"We were both a lot smaller, but I was wiry and when I get mad the adrenalin really takes over."

"Was your mother *really* a bag lady?" Justin asked.

Fred and I responded together, "Justin!" and my brother went back to eating his french fries.

"So Beefy's been trying to beat you up for six years?" I asked.

"Off and on," Fred replied, as if having a guy wanting to beat you up was no more unusual than having a rainy day outside. "It got worse about a year ago. Remember that toilet I booby-trapped?"

"Yeah."

"Guess who used it." Fred had that crazy smile again.

"Beefy?" I asked.

"Yeah. It didn't work quite as well as I hoped, but he still got really drenched. The police got me 'cause I was laughing so much."

"That's funny!" Justin said.

"Not really," Fred told him. "Mostly it was dumb. I'm a lot more mature than I was back then though."

"I'd say you still have a lot of insecurity and latent aggression," I said.

"What?" Fred shot back, staring at me.

"He doesn't know what it *means*, Fred," Justin said. "He just learned it from my dad."

"You kids are incredible. Jason, I think you could be a bank president *or* a psychologist."

"Sure I could," I told him. "But bank presidents make a lot more money."

Chapter 8

Fred brought us back at eleven, a full hour after we were supposed to be in bed. It had taken us quite a while to eat the fries and onion rings. And it took forever to listen while Fred sang two weird songs. I kept reminding Fred during the second song that it was our bedtime, but Justin kept asking him to sing the song again.

So we were late getting home. We were so late that Fred told us to go to sleep "instantly." But nobody can fall asleep right away. That's why I was still wide awake when the door opened downstairs. I could hear my mother's high heels on the front hall floor. Justin was on the top bunk, snoring, so I knew he wasn't asleep either.

"Justin," I whispered.

"I'm asleep," he whispered back.

"No, you're not," I told him. "Cut out the fake snoring."

"It'll fool Mom and Dad. They'll think I'm asleep," he said.

"Justin, you couldn't fool anybody. Besides, you never snore when you're really asleep."

"What do I do?"

"Nothing."

"Then I'll do nothing. Shhh. Here they come."

As they came up the stairs, Fred was explaining to my parents that we had gone out for a snack and my mother was sounding suspicious. I think she wanted to check that we hadn't been damaged by the truck or poisoned by the food.

I kept my eyes closed when she came in the room, though I could feel the hall light on my eyelids. Mom came over to the bunk beds and bent down by me, brushing the hair from my forehead and kissing me goodnight. I just kept my eyes shut tight and tried to breathe slow and easy.

I guess my imitation of sleep worked well enough, because she left my bunk and looked up at Justin. He had stopped the snoring and seemed to be perfectly still, as if he were pretending not just to be asleep but to be dead. Mom gave him a kiss and I heard Justin roll over in bed. He must have opened his eyes, because I heard Mom say, "Did I wake you up, dear?"

"Ummm," Justin said sleepily. "Mom, Fred's the best babysitter ever."

"That's nice. Now go back to sleep."

"Can he babysit us again?" Justin asked.

"We'll see, dear. We'll see," my mother whispered, walking softly toward the door.

"He's the best ever," Justin said, and then seemed to fall off to sleep.

My mother blew us a kiss and closed the bedroom door. I tried to keep the grin on my face under control.

"You were great, Justin. You even fooled me," I whispered.

But my brother was already asleep — for real, this time.

The next morning, there was some serious talk between my parents about Fred. Mom said that he should never have taken us out without asking first, that the truck was unsafe, that we could have been killed or hurt. She left out poisoned, but I didn't feel like helping out her side of the argument. Dad said that Andrew, the minister's son, had taken us to a movie with no objection from her, that Fred's truck was no worse than our rusty Volvo, and that neither of us had been hurt or killed.

"What's more," he pointed out, "Fred has been quite honest about everything he did."

"I don't care," Mom said. "I don't want to use him as a regular babysitter."

"But, dear —" my father said.

"But, Mom —" I said.

Neither of us had the least effect on her. It was Justin who won the day for our side. He didn't try to convince her, or plead with her, or do anything intelligent. He just cried.

"I want Fred," he cried. Big tears ran down his cheeks, and when Mom tried to put her arm around him, he shook her off. "I want *Fred*."

After ten minutes of this, Mom gave in.

Fred became one of our regular babysitters, joining Lisa and Mrs. McCutcheon on the list by the telephone. Lisa still got most of the daytime jobs because she lived up the street and Mom thought she was "dependable." Mrs. McCutcheon got the long babysits because she was almost two hundred years old and was "trustworthy." That didn't leave much for Fred.

We waited just over a week before we broke the truth to Mom. We explained that Lisa spent her babysitting time making out with a kid named Roger on the front couch. And we told her about the time we caught Mrs. McCutcheon taking a drink of Scotch from a bottle in the kitchen and filling it back up with water so it looked like none was missing.

Suddenly Fred went to the top of the babysitter list. Mom started to say things like, "He may look like a juvenile delinquent, but he's reliable and the kids love him."

Now I wasn't sure about the last part of that. Justin and I did like Fred a lot, and we thought he was funny, and maybe we were even fond of him. But I wasn't sure that we loved him. Not then anyhow.

Fred babysat us a lot that summer. We didn't always go out in his truck. Sometimes we'd sit around the house and Fred would sing his terrible songs to us, or he'd show Justin how to catch butterflies and suffocate them in jars, or he'd make up stories that starred Justin and me.

But the best times were when we went out in the truck. Fred would take us cruising downtown to look at the winos on lower James Street. He shouted "why-no!" at them as we drove by so the "why" came out high and the "no" came out low. Another time he took us to the new city jail, walked up to the front door and asked for a tour. The guard stared at us as if we had just escaped from the funny farm. So Fred asked to see the superintendent and told him he was the son of the mayor and wanted to see the facilities. The superintendent took one look at Fred and knew he was getting a line, but when Justin said, "Please can we see the jail?" the old guy gave in and took us around. It was a great jail — TV sets and nice beds and shops and a big gym. Fred kept telling us he'd be better off in there than living with his brother.

"But then you couldn't be our baby-sitter," Justin said, upset.

"Well, that settles it," Fred told him. "I'll be careful to stay on the right side of the law."

And he stayed on that side all summer. My father had made Fred one of his "projects" and maybe that helped him. Dad was a teacher, so he made people his "projects" the way a normal father might refinish a bookshelf or restore a car. Dad preferred to do restoration on people — and Fred was close at hand. By the end of the summer Fred's clothes didn't look quite so weird, his hair had some kind of style, and he'd given up wearing his baseball cap. He even went out on a date, so I guess he improved his lines after that night at McDonald's. Fred had made a lot of progress, or so my father said.

And he seemed happy enough. He delivered manure and babysat us, putting money away in the bank. I suggested he get into the stock market, but he was chicken. In fact, Fred was chicken about a lot of things. The day he was going to visit his mother, for instance, he stalled and whined like Justin going to the dentist. I guess Fred's visit didn't work out so well because my father couldn't talk him into going back for a second try. Maybe his mother really was a bag lady.

But Fred's problems with his mother were nothing compared with the ones he had with Beefy. Beefy had a gang that picked on Fred like Roger Samson bounces a basketball — up and down, over and over.

One day that summer Fred found his truck with paint sprayed all over one side. My father said it must be really bad when kids couldn't even spell swear words properly.

Of course the paint job couldn't be legally blamed on Beefy — but *we* knew. Just as we knew who stole Fred's clothes that day at the beach. And who painted his name on top of the Dundas water tower.

But Fred never seemed to do anything about Beefy. Justin kept on saying he should beat him up, but Justin is big on simple solutions. I advised him to file legal charges, to have a lawyer send Beefy a letter, to seek protection from the local Mafia. But Fred took none of my suggestions. If he had, maybe he would still have had his eyebrows when school started in September.

Chapter 9

Justin was the first to see that there was something wrong with Fred's face. "Look, Jay-Jay," he said as Fred got out of his truck. "Fred hasn't got any eyebrows!"

"I don't want to talk about it," Fred told us as he walked up the stairs. "Don't you dare say a thing." He was staring hard at the two of us.

"A thing!" Justin said.

Fred just shook his fist at him. Then he picked my brother up and put him on his shoulders. Justin always liked this kind of ride and was kept busy yelling and screaming as Fred threatened to walk him into the doorway. As for me, I was still wondering what had happened to Fred's eyebrows.

Fred and Justin got into the front hall as my parents were coming down the stairs. I don't think my father even noticed the change in Fred, but then his brain is often in California. My mother didn't pay much attention either, except just before she went out, when she stared a little longer at his face than usual. Of course she didn't say anything. No polite, civilized person would say anything.

But that didn't include Justin. "Fred," he began, biting his thumb and trying hard to look cute and dumb.

"Yeah," Fred replied. He looked a little upset, but maybe that's how anyone would look without eyebrows.

"How'd you lose them?" Justin asked.

"Justin," I lectured. After all, Fred had told us he didn't want to talk about it.

"Did you go bald, like Daddy?" Justin asked, ignoring me.

"People don't go bald in the eyebrows, Justin," I told him.

"You don't know everything, Jason. *Did* you?" he asked again, looking hard at the skin where Fred's eyebrows used to be.

"No, I went swimming in the bay and they were licked off by a shark."

"Really?" Justin demanded, wide-eyed.

"He's just kidding you," I said. Everybody knows there are no sharks in the bay.

"No, not really," Fred admitted. "The whole thing is just so stupid I don't want to talk about it. Suppose I buy you guys a doughnut. Will you promise not to mention one more word about my eyebrows tonight? Please?"

"Fair deal," I said.

"I promise," Justin said, but I could tell from the grin on his face that he had something crossed — his toes or his fingers or something. "Can I have two maple dips?"

"Who's paying, Fred?" I asked.

"I am. We're celebrating my new job. I'm working part-time at a fish restaurant downtown."

"Are you the fish?" I asked.

"Very funny. Very funny. Sign the kid up and put him on at Yuk Yuk's and see if they throw food at him."

"What *are* you, Fred?" Justin asked.

"I'm a waiter. Fifteen hours a week and real money!" he said, smiling from ear to ear, or from non-eyebrow to non-eyebrow.

"What about your manure business?" I asked him.

"Not one more shovelful," Fred told us. "I won't have time anymore."

"Does that mean you won't have time to babysit us anymore?" Justin asked. He looked really upset and even I got a little worried when I thought about it.

"Don't worry," Fred told him. "I'll still have lots of time free to be with you guys. You're almost like — well, family — real family."

There was an awkward silence at that point. I guess we had all grown pretty close over the last couple months, but nobody had said it out loud before.

"Anyhow, don't get upset. You can have two maple dips, Justin. And Jason, you can have a chocolate éclair. And me, I'm going to have The Special."

Justin's eyes lit up. "The Special," he sighed. "Can I have some of it too?"

"You can have one yourself, if you want."

"Oh boy," Justin breathed. His mind forgot about Fred and his job and his eyebrows. Now it was fixed on the largest cream-filled doughnut that man had ever created. The Special was to regular doughnuts what a submarine was to regular sandwiches. And Fred had just promised to buy two of them!

I think all three of us were dreaming of doughnuts as we climbed into Fred's truck and headed for Tiny Tim's Donut World on the other side of the park. Doughnuts with cream and chocolate and cherry stuff and a sprinkling of nuts —

my stomach was growling just imagining them.

We got into Tiny Tim's and Fred ordered the two Specials and my chocolate éclair. I thought about having a Special myself, but somebody had to be reasonable. Sometimes I wondered why it always turned out to be me.

The doughnuts had just been placed in a large box when we heard the sound.

Bzzzzz.

It didn't make any sense to me. I was busy watching the doughnut box so it wouldn't fall and get them all mushed. Fred was busy paying the girl at the counter.

Bzzzzz.

"Fred," Justin said, "some guy over there is buzzing you."

Fred and I both turned. There was Beefy sitting at a table with three other teenagers.

"Hey, buzzbrows," one of them called out.

"*Bzzzzz,*" said the others.

"His name is Fred," Justin told them.

Fred himself just looked as if he wanted to crawl in the doughnut box and hide.

"*Bzzzzz,*" said Beefy, standing up and walking over just like King Kong Bundy.

"He sounds like a bee," Justin said, laughing. I'm always amazed at how Justin can fail to see the seriousness of a situation.

"It's not a bee, kid," Beefy said. "It's an electric shaver. Just ask buzzbrows to tell you about it. Ask him what happened to his eyebrows."

"What happened to your eyebrows, Fred?" Justin asked.

"Come on, let's get out of here," Fred replied. He grabbed the box of doughnuts and began steering the two of us toward the door.

"I don't know why we have to leave," Justin said.

"I'll explain it all to you when you're seven," I said, pulling on his arm.

Justin thought that was a pretty stupid answer and he was right, but it did the job. The three of us got back to the truck with no more discussion.

"Okay, Ralph baby, now let's get out of here," Fred muttered as we climbed in.

"Who's Ralph?" Justin asked.

"The truck."

"You named your truck Ralph?" I asked him.

"Yeah, last night. It was the only name I could think of that's dumber than Fred."

Fred turned the key and the starter ground and ground, but nothing happened. Fred was turning red in the face.

Over at the doughnut shop, Beefy and his three friends had come out to the door. Together they looked like a small football team — not small in size, but small in number.

Fred tried to start the truck again. He pumped up and down on the gas pedal as the motor made a *grrr*-ing sound like a grizzly bear. It didn't work.

"What's the matter, buzzbrows? Your old rust bucket won't go?" Beefy shouted.

Fred was turning such a bright red that I could honestly compare his cheeks to a tomato. It wouldn't be nice, but I could do it.

"You always forget the magic word," Justin told him. He was busy opening the doughnut box and aiming a Special at his mouth.

"Outrageous curmudgeon," Fred tried. Nothing happened.

"Ragu spaghetti sauce," Justin said calmly, then stuffed his mouth with doughnut. Of course it worked.

Fred raced the engine for a second, then threw the truck into reverse.

"Watch out for my car!" Beefy yelled from Tiny Tim's.

It would have been hard at that point to watch out for anything. Ralph, the truck, had surrounded itself and us with a cloud of oily smoke. I couldn't see a thing. I doubt that Fred could see much more as he backed up.

Bump!

"Fred, we hit something," Justin said. Actually, I think Fred already knew we had hit something.

"You hit my car!" I heard from outside the cloud of smoke. The voice was Beefy's.

Fred put the truck into first gear and pulled forward. There was another awful sound — of metal twisting.

Screeech-clunk!

"This is fun," Justin said. "Do it again, Fred."

Gradually the smoke cleared away and we saw the damage. Fred had hooked bumpers with Beefy's car — that's what made the first bump. And when he had pulled forward, the back bumper on his truck had pulled right off — that had made the screech.

"You ruined my car!" Beefy cried.

"There's not even a scratch," Fred

shouted back, and that was the truth. As far as I could tell, Fred's truck had taken all the damage. As a matter of fact, Fred's truck had taken a lot of damage. But this didn't seem to be a good time for a nice, quiet discussion of the problem.

"I'm gonna kill you!" Beefy shouted.

"Over my dead body," Fred yelled back. Fred was a little upset at this point and not making too much sense. Of course he had reasons to be upset. He now had no bumper on his truck, four guys ready to kill him, two kids to babysit, and his doughnut, a Special, on the floor of the cab.

"Let's get out of here," Fred said to no one in particular. He put the truck into gear and raced back onto Main Street.

"Fred," Justin said.

"Could you just shut up for a while?"

"Your doughnut is down on the floor," Justin told him anyhow.

"Great. Just great. Things couldn't be worse."

"Oh yes, they could," I said after a look out the back window.

"How?"

"Beefy and his friends are following us."

Chapter 10

"Fred, you don't have to run away from them," I said.

"You tell that to the four guys back there in the Camaro."

We were zooming down Main Street about as fast as the traffic and the stoplights would let us. The Camaro with Beefy and his friends was about a block behind us, and gaining. I suppose it would have been worse if we'd been on an open road, like those chase scenes in the movies, but the other traffic kept the Camaro from moving in on us too quickly. I figured our chances of outrunning the Camaro in Fred's rusty old truck were about the same as God actually returning one of Fred's phone calls.

"Fred," I told him, "it's *your* truck that's been damaged. You don't even have to report an accident where the damage is less than five hundred dollars."

"Are you going to be a psychologist, a bank president *and* a lawyer?" he asked.

"I'm serious. You didn't even scratch the paint on his car. The only damage was your bumper."

"That was funny," Justin said. "It made a really big *screwwcch*." He tried to imitate the noise of the bumper pulling off and did a pretty good job of it.

"If there wasn't any damage to Beefy's car," Fred asked, "why is he following us?"

"Maybe he wants to return your bumper?" I suggested limply.

Fred just shot me a look.

"If that Beefy guy tries to hurt you," Justin said in his tough voice, "I'll beat him up."

"Thanks, Justin," Fred replied, though he didn't look very reassured.

"We'd *both* protect Fred, wouldn't we, Jay-Jay?" Justin asked.

"Speak for yourself," I told him.

While I was quite sure that we had every legal right to go about our business, I think Fred might have had a point. Beefy was probably not too concerned about our legal rights. Since the four of them outweighed the three of us by at least a couple tonnes, maybe the best thing for us was to get away from them.

"Can't you go any faster?" I asked Fred. Beefy's Camaro was about half a block behind us now.

"Sure, just tell all these cars to move right off the street or give me a siren so I can play ambulance."

"We've got Justin," I said.

Fred and I both thought about having Justin do a siren imitation at the top of his lungs, but we both reached the same conclusion. "Naah."

"How about we try to lose them," I said. That's a line you hear a lot on TV and it always seems to work for them. I wasn't so sure how it would work in real life.

"Not a bad idea," Fred said, turning the steering wheel hard to the left. He drove half a block, made a right turn into an alley, then a left turn up another alley, roared up a little hill covered with grass, and finally shut off the motor when we came to a halt beside a big garbage bin.

"Hey, I know where we are," I told him.

"It's our school," Justin shouted out.

"Shhh! I think we lost them, but if you two keep on yelling like that they can home in on the noise."

"Sorry," I whispered, though it was Justin who was the problem.

We waited in silence for a minute or two. It was pretty tense. It occurred to me that I really needed to go to the washroom, but I figured this was the wrong time to mention it.

After a while Fred climbed out the window on his side of the truck and went out on the hood. Then he peeked over the top of the garbage bin, ducking his head back down after a second.

"You two get down," he whispered.

"Get down where?" I whispered back.

"Down on the floor so they can't see you. I'm going to scout around to see if we can make a break for your place."

I wasn't too happy about getting on the floor with the remains of Fred's doughnut, but Justin had already climbed under the dashboard and seemed very pleased with all the excitement.

"This is fun!"

"Oh, yeah," I whispered.

"But this truck smells like poo," he said with a giggle.

"It's manure, Justin. Manure."

But the smell was the same regardless of what I called it. Now that the truck had stopped, it was really beginning to build up. And it was starting to get to me. I hadn't even begun to eat my chocolate éclair, and my stomach had already reached its limit.

"Fred!" I called in a loud whisper. I even raised my head over the dashboard to see where he was.

"What do you want?" Fred asked. He had just turned to get back into the truck.

"I'm going to throw up," I told him.

"What?"

I put my hand over my mouth. I couldn't talk about it anymore or I'd do it.

"He said he's going to toss his cookies," Justin explained for me.

"Hang your head out the window if you have to," Fred whispered. "Or better yet, hold it until we get to a bathroom."

"Can't we go home?" I asked.

"Beefy's Camaro is parked just down the street from your house," Fred told me. "But there's nobody in it."

"I want to go to *your* house, Fred," Justin said.

"Some other night," Fred told him,

climbing back into the cab through the window on the driver's side.

"Why can't we?"

"Beefy knows where I live."

"*Please*, Fred."

This stupid little exchange took our attention away from the real problem. Justin was getting very whiny, as if Fred's brother's house was such a treat that we should risk our lives to get there. Fred was pointing out, and he was right, that we'd been to his house lots of times and had no particular reason to go there right away. I was busy trying to keep my stomach under control.

Then we heard it.

"Buzzbrows. *Bzzzz. Bzzzz.*"

The three of us looked out and saw Beefy and his friends surrounding the truck.

Did we ever move in a hurry! Fred turned the key, Justin yelled "Ragu spaghetti sauce," the truck roared into life, and Fred threw it into reverse.

Beefy's two friends behind the truck

went running for their lives as Fred bounced back down the grassy hill. Then we were twisting through the alleys to get to the street.

We were okay for the time being. We had only one immediate problem now. Mine.

"Geez," Fred cried. "Didn't I tell you to hang your head out the window if you couldn't hold it?"

Chapter 11

"How do you feel now?" Fred asked me.

"Better," I said. As long as I didn't look at the floor of the truck, I felt fine.

"The smell of your truck made Jay-Jay sick," Justin lectured.

"The smell of manure does not make people sick," Fred answered. "In fact, one of your ancestors liked the smell so much he built pipes from the stable to his bedroom just so he could smell the manure when he went to sleep."

"Ugh!" Justin made a face.

"Really?" I asked.

"That's what your father told me."

"I always wondered what he talked about in his English classes," I said.

"Too bad he didn't do a lesson on where to go when somebody wants to mash your face," Fred sighed. "We can't go to your house and we better not go to mine. How about we go to LaSalle Park and I'll show you guys how I can hypnotize trees and make them fall asleep?"

"You already showed us that one, Fred," Justin replied.

"Well, what say we go to the lift bridge and I'll do my famous imitation of a German submarine firing torpedos?"

"You did that one too," I reminded him. "And I had to rescue you before you drowned in the canal."

"Oh, yeah, I remember that now." Fred was really racking his brain trying to come up with something new. "Okay, then, let's go see a drive-in movie just to kill some time. Then we can head back to your place when the coast is clear," he suggested.

"Do you have any money left after the doughnuts?" I asked him.

"Uh — no," he said.

"Then do you have a line of credit at some movie theatre, or am I supposed to bail you out again?"

"Ah, asked just like a bank president," Fred told me, grinning. I think the wheels and gears in his brain were busy whirring around.

"Well?" I asked.

"Trust me," he replied, pointing to where his eyebrows should have been. "We're off to the movies."

"I wanna see *The Shaggy D.A.*," Justin said.

"That hasn't been playing for at least a year," I told him.

"You don't know *everything*, Jason," he shot back. "Can we, Fred? Can we?"

"I don't know, Justin. Suppose we go up to the drive-in and take potluck," Fred replied.

"I don't want to see *Potluck*. I wanna see *The Shaggy D.A.*"

Fred just shook his head and kept driving. I think he'd been Justin-ed out at last.

When we got up the mountain to the drive-in I was still waiting to find out how Fred was going to get us past the ticket booth without paying. The answer was simple — he didn't drive anywhere near the ticket booth. He steered the truck way down the road past the movie. Then he put it halfway into a ditch before finally turning it off.

"You guys just follow behind me," he instructed. "I'll bring the blanket. Jason, you bring whatever money you've got so we can get some popcorn. And Justin, you bring yourself and don't get lost. Got it?" Fred looked sternly at us.

"Got it."

"Got it."

I never realized before how dark it is out in the country without any street lights. There was a bit of light reflected from the movie screen and some from the moon, but we still couldn't see much.

Fred led the way. I followed him and Justin followed me. We were doing pretty well, except for bumping into each other in the dark, when from somewhere close by I heard a dog bark.

"Fred, it's a dog," I whispered, frozen in my tracks.

"Ouch," Justin said, bumping into me. "Tell me when you're going to stop."

"Shhh!" Fred shushed. "Don't worry. Come on."

I did worry, but I followed him anyhow. I could just imagine a Great Dane zooming out of the dark and eating all three of us. My mother would have a fit.

"Ick!" Fred whispered.

"What's the matter?" I asked, stopping so Justin ran into me again.

"I stepped in some dog p— uh — manure," Fred whispered. Justin started giggling. He's still at the stage where that kind of thing seems pretty funny.

Fred took some time to wipe his foot on the grass. Then all three of us walked on toward the movie screen, carefully watching where our feet were stepping. That doesn't mean we could actually see anything in the dark, but we were trying.

We finally came to the parking area of the drive-in and settled down next to one of the back speaker posts. Fred spread the blanket down on the ground and the three of us sat with the speaker propped on Fred's shoulder.

"Fred, are you sure you wiped your foot off?" I asked.

"Yes, I'm sure."

"I think I smell something."

"Would you just shut up and watch the movie," Fred whispered.

That seemed like a good idea. It was *Revenge of the Pink Panther* and we were just at the part where the big karate guy falls through all the floors in Clouseau's apartment building. The scene is pretty funny and it made me laugh, especially when the guy ended up in cement. I glanced at Fred and saw he was enjoying it too.

But Justin wasn't happy. "I'm cold," he whined.

"Put the blanket over your shoulders and move in between us. You'll warm up," Fred suggested.

"And I'm hungry."

"How about it, Jason?" Fred asked. "I'm almost broke."

"How come I always have to rescue us from *your* financial problems?" I asked.

"How about we share one big box of popcorn? Have you got enough for that?" Fred asked, ignoring my question.

"Well . . ."

"Don't be such a cheapskate, Jason," Justin said in a loud voice.

He was answered by a voice from a car up ahead of us. "You kids better shut up or I'll get the manager!"

"Uh-oh," I whispered.

"Shhh," Fred shushed again.

We sat and watched the movie in silence. Clouseau's car was busy falling apart. The hood sprang up, the doors fell open and the roof lifted off while the car vibrated up and down. I punched Fred's arm. "That's just like your truck."

"I *like* Fred's truck," Justin broke in.

"So do I. I'm just saying that Clouseau's car is sort of funny like Fred's truck."

"Don't make fun of Fred's truck," Justin said.

"I didn't."

"You *did*."

"No, I didn't."

"Shhh. Now you've done it," Fred cut us off.

We could all see a guy from the projection booth walking back with a flashlight. At first I tried to convince myself he wasn't coming for us, but the closer he came the more scared I got. When he was about two rows away, Fred stood up.

"Exit stage right," he whispered, pulling the blanket out from under us.

"This is your fault," I said to Justin.

I think he stuck his tongue out at me, but it was so dark I couldn't tell for sure. Besides, I was too scared to worry about it. I could just see my parents having to pick us up at the police station after the guy had us arrested.

We left the drive-in a lot faster than

we'd come in. I was more worried about the guy from the projection booth than about anything on the ground, and I was following right behind Fred — too close behind him.

"Oof," I said, bumping into him when he stopped.

"Watch it, will you?" Fred whispered. "Where's Justin?"

"I don't know. He was following me," I said.

We stood in the middle of the field trying to see Justin's shadow against the light of the screen. Nothing. Then we looked in the other direction, but couldn't see much in the dark.

"Oh, great," Fred moaned, knowing we were in real trouble.

"Justin," I half yelled and half whispered.

Fred started to do the same. "Justin . . . Justin!"

We were getting pretty desperate by this time. It was one thing to almost get caught by the manager of a drive-in, but it was a lot worse to lose your six-year-old brother in a field in the middle of the night. I started feeling sick again.

Then a horn beeped out *ahyouga* off by the road. Fred stood still.

"Somebody's beeping my horn," he told me.

"Beefy?" I wondered.

The horn *ahyougad* again — five short blasts. Nobody over the age of seven would beep a horn like that.

"Justin!" Fred cried.

A second later we were racing through the field back toward the pickup. And there was Justin sitting behind the wheel of Fred's truck, grinning like crazy.

"You guys are so slow," he laughed.

"It's not funny, Justin," I said quite seriously.

Justin stuck out his tongue at me and hit the horn button again. *Ahyouga.*

"Would you stop that!" Fred yelled. "You're going to wake up the people with the dog. Come on, we'd better get out of here."

The two of us climbed into the truck. Justin was sandwiched between Fred and me and didn't seem too happy with that spot. He made a face and pointed to Fred's shoes, but I decided he was exaggerating again. I couldn't smell anything worse than what was already on the floor of the truck.

"Let's head back to your house," Fred sighed. I think even he was tired by this time.

"And you can tell us what happened to your eyebrows," I reminded him.

"Do I have to?"

"Yes!" Justin and I said together, just to make it perfectly clear.

So Fred began his story.

Chapter 12

"My eyebrows —" Fred began.

"A shark ate 'em," Justin interrupted. "With one big slurp."

"He was just kidding when he said that, Justin."

"You mean a shark didn't eat 'em?" Justin asked Fred.

"No," Fred admitted. "To tell you the truth, Justin, I've never seen a shark up close."

"Awwwh," Justin replied, his voice so disappointed it even made me feel bad.

"The real story is about my own stupidity. It's hard to believe I actually got involved with all that again. Your dad keeps on saying how much progress I've made, and when I think about how stupid I was — well, I might as well give up and go back to being a juvenile dinkent again."

"Don't give up, Fred," I told him, trying to make him feel better. After all, there are worse things than losing your eyebrows.

"Besides, Fred, it's juvenile *delinquent*," Justin said. "And you don't want to be one of those."

Fred and I both stared at him. I don't think we'd ever heard him say the word correctly before.

"Get on with the story, Fred," Justin prompted. "You should start it 'Once upon a time,' just like all your other stories."

"Okay. Once upon a time, like Tuesday, I was riding the King Street bus going downtown when I noticed these two beautiful girls giving me the eye. Now that didn't surprise me much because I'm actually a handsome prince in disguise as a teenage weirdo. Also, I'm just dynamite with women."

"Oh, sure, sure," I commented.

"So I started talking to the girls, and the next thing you know they invited me to their place. I know it was stupid to go, Jason, so you don't have to tell me. But I went anyhow — maybe it was the juvenile delinquent in me — and there was this party going on. So I got busy trying to impress the girls with just how suave and sophisticated I am, but I ended up drinking a little too much and — uh —"

"You got drunk," Justin suggested.

"Yeah, that's right. So there I was, drunk — but still suave and sophisticated."

"What's swab mean?" Justin broke in. "Is that like a Q-tip?"

"It means the same as sophisticated," I told him.

"So why would Fred say he was sophisticated and sophisticated?"

"Because it sounds better in French," Fred explained. "Now let me finish the story. Did I mention that Beefy was at the party?"

"I figured he might be part of this," I said.

"You're right. Anyway, I was busy

drinking and making a fool of myself when all of a sudden . . ." He paused dramatically.

"What?" Justin asked.

"I passed out. The last thing I remember was telling one of the girls that TV had turned her brain to cauliflower. The next thing I knew, I woke up and everybody was laughing at me. At first I didn't know what it was all about. Then I went into the bathroom and saw the damage."

"Bye-bye eyebrows," I said.

"They shaved 'em right off," Fred agreed. "I'm sure it was Beefy, but nobody would admit it."

"Did you get real mad and go back and beat everybody up?" Justin asked, wide-eyed.

"Not exactly. I got real mad, all right, so I went up to Beefy and the girls and I — uh — I gave them a lecture about respect for human beings and all that."

"What did they do?"

"They laughed."

"That's terrible," Justin said, getting mad on Fred's behalf. "I'd have punched them all right in the nose. I think you're just scared of them." Justin looked at Fred as if he were really disappointed in him.

"You don't prove courage by punching people, Justin," I told him. "It's got to be inside you."

"Well, I don't like Beefy at all. I don't like *any* teenagers. Except you, Fred. Even if you are chicken."

"Thanks a lot." Fred sighed.

Fred was driving the truck onto our street when I spotted a Camaro parked there.

"Fred, don't stop the truck," I said quickly.

"Huh?" Fred had been really quiet since Justin called him a chicken.

"See that Camaro down there?" I said, pointing in front of the old Captain's house. "Isn't that —"

"Not again!" Fred cried.

It was too late to get away. Beefy and his friends had already seen Fred's truck. As we made a big U-turn on the street, the lights of the Camaro came on.

"How come we're going in circles, Fred?" Justin asked.

"It's good for my health," Fred told him. "That's Beefy in the car back there. Anybody who'd wait around for two hours to beat me up must have something really swell in mind."

"Well, if he tries to hurt you, I'm gonna punch him right in the —"

"Nose," I suggested.

"No, right in the you-know-where, Jason. I'm too little to reach his nose."

Fred and I both looked over at Justin. Every so often the workings of his six-year-old brain managed to impress us both.

"Fred, they're right behind us," I announced.

"Got any good ideas?" he asked.

"What you need is a stunt man, not a lawyer or a bank president," I said.

"I wanna be a stunt man," Justin broke in. "You wanna see me jump out of the truck?"

"No!" Fred shouted. "Jason, lock the door."

I locked the door to keep Justin from trying anything heroic but dumb.

"Where are the cops when you need them?" Fred complained loudly, something my mother does a lot when she goes out driving.

"Maybe if the police won't come to us, we should go to them," I suggested.

"What?" Fred asked. He was busy watching Beefy's Camaro in the rearview mirror.

"Just drive over to the police station downtown," I said. "Beefy would never dare to follow us inside their parking lot, and then we'd have somebody to protect us on the way home."

"Not a bad idea for a ten-year-old kid," Fred told me.

"Ten-and-three-quarters," I corrected.

Fred made a quick turn up to Lawrence Road and then bounced along to the west. Lawrence Road has more potholes than any other street in town and they made Fred's truck bounce and shake like an old washing machine.

"How're we doing?" Fred asked.

"Beefy had to slow down," I told him. "But he's still close."

"I'll speed up when the road gets better," Fred replied.

Unfortunately, so did Beefy. Again I tried to calculate the chances of Fred's prehistoric truck actually outracing Beefy's Camaro on a smooth road. I kept on coming up with zero.

But Fred was trying hard. We were really zooming along a little street that headed south when everything went crazy. Fred's truck jumped up in the air, came back down, hit something else, bounced up, crashed down.

"This is f-f-fun," Justin shouted, though I think he was more scared than anything else. So was I.

"W-w-what's doing th-this?"

"I forgot the railroad tracks," Fred shouted.

He had to shout because of the awful scraping noise the Camaro was making behind us. It sounded like those screaming elephants you see in Tarzan movies — only louder.

The truck finally reached some smooth road beyond the railroad crossing. But the Camaro was no longer behind us. It was still sitting on the railroad tracks.

"What happened?" Justin asked as Fred pulled the truck over to the side of the road.

"I think their rear axle got pulled off. Or maybe the transmission broke," Fred explained.

"How come Beefy is still in the car?" Justin asked.

A better question would have been why *nobody* was getting out of the car. It occurred to me that the Camaro had just made a very quick stop from a very high speed — sort of like hitting a brick wall in the middle of a street.

"Those guys could be really hurt, Fred," I pointed out.

"I'm glad that Beefy guy is hurt. He *deserves* it," Justin pronounced.

"Justin," Fred and I said together.

I think we would both have lectured him about respect for human beings and all that, but there wasn't time. At that moment the red crossing lights started flashing and the wooden barriers began to come down across the road. For a few seconds all of us were frozen, even Justin, who probably didn't even understand what might happen. We kept watching the Camaro, waiting for somebody to get out.

Finally the back passenger door opened and one of the four guys staggered away from the car. Then there was no more movement.

The crossing signals kept flashing and a bell was ringing. In the distance we could hear the train approaching.

There were other people in other cars backed up at the crossing now, but none of them was making any move to help the guys in the Camaro.

"Is the train gonna hit them, Fred?" Justin asked.

"There are three sets of tracks," Fred told him. "The train could go right by."

"Or it could smash right into them," I said. "You better do something."

"Why me? I'm just your average juvenile delinquent."

"No, you're *not*, Fred," Justin told him, sounding quite serious.

"But I don't even like Beefy," he said.

"That doesn't matter," I told him. "Unless you really are chicken."

Fred looked at Justin and me, took about half a second to think it over, then scrambled over us out of the truck and back to the crossing.

"Is there gonna be a big crash?" Justin asked.

"Maybe," I told him, "but it will definitely not be fun."

We could see Fred pulling Beefy from the car, then a passenger from the back seat. There was another man working on the other side of the car, helping the last person out. The flashing red lights made them look like robots, moving jerkily as they dragged the teenagers away from the crossing.

I was hoping the train might see the car on the tracks and slow down, but the light just kept coming closer. We could hear the whistle now, bellowing to get Beefy's car off the tracks.

Beefy and his friends were safely clear of the car by now. Fred and the other man were standing with them as the train approached. The whistle was blowing like crazy.

"Should I close my eyes?" Justin asked at the last minute.

It was too late for me to give him advice. The train finally put on its brakes when the engineer saw that the car on the tracks wasn't moving, but it was too late. The engine slid into the crossing with its wheels screeching and sparks shooting from the tracks.

Then it hit.

The Camaro bounced away from the train at first, then spun around and got hit again as the train kept coming. When the train finally stopped, quite a way down the track, the Camaro was wrapped around its front end like a squashed hotdog.

"That was *something!*" Justin said.

"I thought you were going to close your eyes."

"I peeked," he explained. "Jay-Jay, when Fred took Beefy and those guys from the car, does that mean he's not chicken?"

"It better," I told to him. "He's going to need a lot of courage to explain all this to Mom and Dad."

Chapter 13

It took us a long time to tell everything to the police. I kept looking at my watch and wondering what my parents must be thinking. My mom has the kind of imagination that just gets started with Justin and me lying bleeding beside a wrecked car. Give her another five minutes and she can imagine a child-molesting homicidal maniac attacking us with hooks and chain saws. By now it was pushing one in the morning. I figured my mother's imagination had gone way beyond hooks and chain saws into things so horrible I don't even know about them yet.

"Fred, we're going to get in trouble," I tried to tell him. He didn't pay much attention to me. He was listening as a policeman congratulated him for the fifth time on saving Beefy's life. Maybe he was too amazed at what he'd done to think about taking us home.

The policeman lectured Beefy and his friends about safe driving and their narrow escape and why they were being charged. Finally the tow truck came to take away the squashed Camaro. Fred still wasn't listening to me. Fortunately the policeman suggested that the three of us go on home — something I'd been saying for half an hour — and Fred agreed. It was almost one-thirty.

My parents had been home since twelve-fifteen.

"Do you have any idea how worried we've been? Can you imagine what's been going through my mind!" my mother said, or screamed, or something in between, as soon as she saw us. It certainly wasn't one of her nicer voices.

And then she started giving Fred The Look, even worse than my dad ever got it. She kept going on so much about how glad she was to have us back alive, and how much she wanted to kill us for staying out so late, that it was hard for anybody to say anything sensible.

My father was at least calm enough to ask Fred and Justin and me to explain what happened. When the whole story came out, he said that what we did was "understandable, given the situation." And then my mother started giving him The Look too.

"Why don't we talk about all this in the morning, dear," Dad said. "The kids are exhausted."

"Don't call me dear," my mother cut in, a line she often uses when she's mad and my father is trying to get on her good side. "*All* of you have a lot to answer for," she accused everybody. But she kept her eyes focused on Fred.

"We can do it tomorrow," my father told her. Now he was looking angry. I could see the two of them were heading for a real fight, but I was too tired to try to head it off.

I can't say whether they actually had a fight or not, because I fell asleep as soon as I hit my bed. When I woke up, it was almost ten in the morning and Justin was still sound asleep. Dad was making some muffins in the kitchen. He told me not to say a word about last night until we had a family conference on the whole thing.

A family conference meant that we were in *real* trouble. My parents didn't call for a family conference on minor problems. You could drop a trayful of dishes on the floor and not have to face a family conference. You could even drop some of my mother's grandmother's antique Limoges on the floor and not have to face the court of the whole family. But when something really went wrong — say when we were going to move to London, or when Justin saw a flasher in Gage Park — then we had a family conference.

"That bad?" I said to my father.

"Yeah," he replied, popping the muffins in the oven.

"Then I think Fred should be at the conference," I announced.

Dad just looked at me as if I were crazy.

"Well, we were all in it together last night," I explained. "And he was the babysitter. And besides, he's almost like part of the family." I paused for a second while all that sunk in. "It would only be fair, Dad," I concluded. My father was really big on fair.

"I guess you're right," he finally agreed.

I was going to say "Of course," but decided against it. I figured that whatever happened during the family conference, it wouldn't be quite so bad if it had to happen in front of Fred. I was also playing for time. I figured that bringing in Fred meant we couldn't do the conference that morning or afternoon. The longer we could put it off, the more my parents would have cooled down.

As it turned out, Fred was working at the fish restaurant that night and

Justin had a birthday party to go to. So the family conference was put off until Sunday night after dinner. That was our first stroke of good luck.

The second came with the evening paper, on page eight. *STUDENTS RESCUED BEFORE FIERY CRASH* ran the headline. Up above was a picture of Beefy's car wrapped around the front of the train. And Fred was right in the first paragraph: a hero.

My father was the one who found the article. He read it out loud to my mother, then had to read it twice more to Justin. Justin was very impressed. He cut the article out for his "collection," as if he actually had a collection of anything besides Dinky cars.

If my mother had been half that impressed, we wouldn't have needed the family conference. But she wasn't. She wasn't ready to be impressed by anything anybody said about Fred. And that's what got me worried.

I guess Justin was worried too. "Jay-

Jay, why do we have to have this conference?" he asked me when we were up in our room.

"Because of Friday night. They're going to use that as an excuse to lay down some new rules," I said.

"Like what?"

"Like no driving around with Fred, maybe. Or no driving around with anybody." I had a hunch it could be worse than that, but I didn't want to tell him unless I had to. Why get him upset?

"That's dumb," he said.

"Parents are dumb a lot of the time. What can you expect?"

"But Fred's a hero," Justin said. "They can't punish us if Fred's a hero."

"Want to make a bet?" I said.

"But it *said*, Jay-Jay."

"I know what it said, Justin. But that doesn't change the fact that we're in deep trouble."

"Really?" Justin asked.

"Up to our knees," I told him.

"What if Mom and Dad are real mad, Jay-Jay? Do you think . . ."

"Think what?"

"Maybe they won't let Fred babysit us anymore. Maybe they won't even let us *see* Fred again. Ever." Justin's voice was cracking.

"That's what I'm really afraid of," I admitted. "I think it's coming."

"Then what are we going to do?" he asked.

"I'll try to talk them out of it," I promised. "But you know what you can do that's even better than that?"

"What?" Justin asked.

"Cry," I told him. "Cry like you've never cried in your whole life."

The next night we had roast chicken for Sunday dinner, just like always. Roast chicken usually cheers everybody up, because it's the only meal we all like to eat. But that night it didn't work. The mood was as thick as the chicken gravy — you could balance a spoon in it. Justin didn't even finish his mashed potatoes, and he *always* finishes mashed potatoes. My mother took his temperature to see if he was all right. But Justin wasn't sick, he was just worried. He had good reason to be.

When Fred came by after dinner, even he looked worried. My father asked him what it was like to be famous and Fred said that, given the choice, he'd rather be rich. But nobody laughed. Nobody even smiled. That's how we were all feeling.

We went out to the kitchen for the family conference. That's where we always have them, maybe because our old apartment didn't have a dining room so there was no place else to sit down and talk. Even now, with thirteen other rooms to choose from, we still go to the kitchen for a family conference. The smell of roast chicken was heavy as we began.

"I suppose you boys all know what this is about," my father said. He always starts a family conference by saying what everybody already knows. "Your mother and I were very upset about what happened on Friday."

I looked at Mom. She was more than upset, she was sitting at the table as if she had turned to stone.

Dad went on. "And we think we should make some changes in the rules so — uh — that kind of thing won't happen again."

I shot a look at Justin to say that my prediction was right, but he wasn't looking at me. He had his eyes fixed on Fred as if he never expected to see him again. Ever.

"If I could say something, sir," Fred chimed in. "I'd like to say that it wasn't really the fault of the boys. We got involved in a chain of events and — well, I guess I have to take the responsibility for what happened."

"We were all part of it, Fred," I told him.

"I think the real question here is one of judgement," my father said. "As you boys get older, we naturally expect you to show better judgement in situations like that."

"And that means," my mother said, breaking her silence, "that you shouldn't get into anything as crazy and dangerous. There's no reason Jason and Justin should have been involved in the problems between you and Beefy," she told Fred.

"I agree with you —" Fred began.

"It wasn't Fred's fault," Justin cut in. "It was just an accident. He didn't make Beefy chase us."

"That's true," I said. I was surprised at how intelligent Justin was being.

"Both of you could have been killed," my mother said.

Then everybody began talking at once. Justin was complaining, Fred was explaining, and my father was trying to keep order. Finally my father raised his voice.

"All right," he shouted, "everybody calm down. We're not having a conference to trade accusations. The question is, where do we go from here? Your mother and I —"

But before he could get started with the verdict, Fred broke in. "Sir, before you say what you have in mind, can I just say a few things? After all, this is largely my fault."

We all got quiet. My father looked over at my mother, then told Fred to go ahead.

"You said before that this was really a question of judgement, and I think you're right. I should have found a better and safer way out of the situation before it got as bad as it did. And I have to apologize about that. I think I made a serious mistake, even if we did come out of it all right. I don't think a babysitter should make that kind of mistake where kids could really get hurt. And that's why I think — well, with this new job at the restaurant and all, I shouldn't be babysitting the boys anymore."

I just stared wide-eyed at Fred. That

was what I'd been expecting from my parents — and here it was coming from Fred!

"But —" I said.

"Well —" my father began.

"I think —" my mother cut in.

But none of us was able to finish because Justin started wailing. He was screaming and crying as if it were the end of the world. The noise in the kitchen was worse than when the train hit Beefy's car.

"Justin," my mother said, reaching over to comfort him.

He shook off her hand, got up from his chair and ran to Fred. He threw his arms around Fred's neck and hugged him for all he was worth. I was afraid, from the pink colour Fred was turning, that Justin had cut off his breathing.

"Justin," Fred said, putting his arm around my brother and hoisting him up on his lap, "that's how it has to be."

Justin was still crying, the tears falling down his cheeks and dripping off his chin. His crying made all of us feel terrible. My father looked as if he'd rather be anywhere else — California, anywhere but here. My mother looked about to cry herself, maybe for other reasons. None of us knew what to do next, except maybe Fred. He was the one who kept on talking while the rest of us were at a loss for words.

"Now, Justin, if you'll listen for a second you'll see it won't be so bad. Just listen," he said, pulling my brother in close. "Even though I'm going to stop babysitting you kids, I'm going to ask your parents for a special privilege."

"What's that?" my father asked.

"I want to keep on being their friend," he said. He was smiling.

"Well, of course," my mother told him.

"But if I'm going to be a friend," Fred explained, "that means I can still visit and the kids can still go places with me in the truck — so long as you give your permission."

My father looked at my mother. I

could see her trying to weigh everything in her mind. She looked over at Justin clutching Fred's neck, and that seemed to help her make a decision. She nodded to my dad.

"I guess that would be all right," she said slowly.

"So we can still see Fred?" Justin asked, wiping his cheeks.

"Sure," Mom agreed.

"And go to McDonald's with him?"

"Yes."

"In the truck?"

"Well, I suppose," she said reluctantly. "So long as you're in at a reasonable hour."

"And we can still go to his house and hear his dumb songs?"

"Yes," my dad said.

"But who's going to babysit me?" Justin asked at last.

"If I could make a suggestion, ma'am," Fred told my mother, "you really don't need an outside babysitter anymore. Jason is the most mature kid

I've ever met in my entire life. There's no reason he couldn't look after Justin by himself, so long as there's a neighbour or someone he can call if there's a problem."

Everybody looked at me. I just smiled. Everything Fred had told them was the simple truth.

"But he's only ten," my father said.

"I'll be eleven in a month," I reminded him.

"Eleven going on forty, sir," Fred said.

My parents both laughed, then Fred and Justin joined in. After that everybody started talking about everything — the accident and the newspaper article and Fred's job at the restaurant. We were finished with the tough part of the family conference.

After a while Fred said that the smell of the roast chicken was too much for him and he asked for some leftovers. My mother started heating some up in the microwave, and Justin asked for more mashed potatoes and gravy. He said he was hungry again. Mom asked why he hadn't been hungry at dinner, then laughed because she knew the answer herself.

Fred finished up half the chicken while Justin went through a pile of potatoes the size of a small mountain. After promising to come by next Wednesday on his night off and sing a new weird song to us, Fred went home.

Justin and I went to bed. I was tired and wanted to sleep, but Justin didn't. I think he was fired up by all the mashed potatoes.

"I don't think *you're* going to be a very good babysitter, Jay-Jay," he said.

"Why not?" I groaned.

"Because you're too boring. All you ever want to do is read a book or watch TV."

"So when I'm babysitting we'll do something else. Maybe I'll play gin rummy with you, if you're good. Now go to sleep."

"And you were wrong, Jay-Jay."

"How's that?"

"You said we weren't going to be able to see Fred anymore, but it didn't happen. So you don't know everything."

"I said it *might* happen, and it almost did. Do you know why it didn't?"

"'Cause I cried?"

"Yeah. And who told you to cry?"

"You did," Justin admitted, thinking about the whole thing. "Maybe you do know one or two things," he said.

I smiled and rolled over in bed. Maybe, for a six-and-a-half-year-old, he wasn't that dumb after all.